DEADLY PERFORMANCE

A DOTTY SAYERS ANTIQUE MYSTERY

VICTORIA TAIT

KANGA PRESS

A Kanga Press Publication © 2023

Cover Design by Daniela Colleo of StunningBookCovers.com
Editing Allie Douglas

For more information visit VictoriaTait.com

CHAPTER ONE

"Meow," wailed Earl Grey pitifully from his black canvas travel carrier wedged under the aeroplane seat.

"It's OK," soothed Dotty Sayers, as much to calm her own beating heart as her distressed British blue cat. She clutched the armrests as the plane lurched, buffeted by turbulence.

All she could see outside were swirling white clouds.

"We're nearly home," she muttered.

But that wasn't really true. Where was her home?

The comfortable little cottage she rented on the edge of Fairford? Fairford was a picturesque Cotswold town in the south-west of England, with houses of honey-coloured stone and the River Coln winding lazily past the tall-steepled church.

It had felt like home for over a year, while she worked nearby at Akemans auction house and antiques centre. But that was before she'd been arrested for murder, released, and then attacked by the real culprit when she realised he was the mastermind behind several deaths and a series of antique frauds.

Southern France wasn't home, but she'd relished the last three months there, growing to love the gentle life on the farm where she'd stayed, and the laughter of the eleven-year-old twin girls she'd been looking after.

She thought of Jean, the girls' grandmother, and her mouth watered. Together they'd created hearty casseroles, delicious soups, and fruity puddings. Her stomach churned as the plane pitched again.

Maybe she should stop thinking about food.

"Meow."

"Please, don't worry," she said kindly, but with a tremor in her voice.

And then the lurching stopped, and the plane levelled out.

Staring out of the window, Dotty gazed down at a patchwork of yellow and brown fields. August in rural England meant harvest time.

She was landing at Newcastle, in the north-east of England, and catching a train to Edinburgh, Scotland's capital city. But that wasn't home either. Her parents had only recently bought a flat there because it was closer to her mum's work and, she suspected, her social life.

Dotty had never visited Edinburgh. No, that wasn't entirely true. In her last monthly call to her dad, he'd told her they were once stationed with the army at the fun sounding Penicuik, next to the Pentland Hills, on the outskirts of the city. But she'd only been a toddler and had no recollection of that.

The smiling air stewardess made steady progress through the cabin, checking passengers' seat belts were secure and asking some to, "Please fold away your tray."

They were preparing to land.

Dotty glanced outside and pressed her lips together in disappointment. It was grey and dull, and looked very wet from recent rainfall. The south of France had been warm and glorious, and she realised she might not have packed enough jumpers for this damp, cool weather.

Maybe it would be different in Edinburgh.

Maybe she'd receive a warm welcome, and be respected as the woman she'd now become, rather than the timid girl who'd left home ten years ago, to marry a man she didn't choose.

CHAPTER TWO

Dotty had messaged her dad to tell him she'd be in Coach J. And there he was, jogging along the platform to keep up with the slowing train.

She saw him eagerly waiting and realised that, if it was possible, he'd board the train and help her disembark. Instead, she waited patiently as the queue of passengers shuffled slowly towards the carriage doors.

"Where's your bag?" called her dad.

She pushed her black suitcase forward and his strong, tattooed arms picked it up. He hadn't changed much since he'd left the army, although he wore his hair even shorter. It was receding and sprinkled with grey, especially above his ears.

She was grateful for his help, and his steadying hand when a young man barged past. In his carrier, Earl Grey meowed pitifully as he was jolted. What must he make of the shrill whistles, the public address system announcing the imminent departure of a train to Glasgow, and the noise of people everywhere?

And there were so many of them. Was everybody descending on Edinburgh?

"Come this way," called her father as he rolled her suitcase, pushing against the tide of people flowing along the concrete platform.

Her father had retained his southern Scottish accent. He'd been brought up in one of the tougher areas of the Borders as he'd so often told her.

A young boy dropped his droopy-eared rabbit as he passed them.

Dotty stopped, picked up the well-loved toy, and searched for its owner.

She saw him tugging his mother's hand as she consulted an electronic information board.

"Here you are," she whispered to the boy as she approached him.

His mother looked round and scowled, so Dotty gave her a weak smile and turned back along the emptying platform.

Hurrying, with Earl Grey's carrier swinging as she did so, she caught up with her dad and said brightly, "Thanks for meeting me."

"Couldn't have you getting mixed up with this lot." He glanced irritably back at the passengers' retreating backs. "Next year, I'm persuading your mother to rent the flat out in August, and we can spend a few quiet weeks in the Borders."

"But what about her work?" asked Dotty as they reached a flight of concrete steps. She didn't ask why her mum hadn't come to meet her. She'd have thought something was very wrong if she had.

Her dad ignored the lift and heaved her suitcase up onto a footbridge which crossed the railway tracks. "She can catch a train, or work from home. I'm fed up with all the tourists. I can't go anywhere without them loitering about in groups or asking me for directions."

They emerged onto a low-level street, passing under a stone arch supporting the road above.

"And she's been fussing ever since you told us you were planning to visit. Buying curtains and new bed linen for your room, and food bowls for your cat. How did he like the journey, by the way?"

"He didn't. I just hope he doesn't run off when I let him out. The city is so different from the fields he's been used to exploring."

The road sloped upwards until they joined a wider, busier street beside a modern-looking shopping centre. They walked along a wide stone pavement between nondescript corporate buildings. It was much cooler than she'd become accustomed to but at least a small patch of blue sky was emerging between the retreating grey clouds.

"It's a ten-minute walk from here, but downhill. Are you OK carrying your cat?"

In truth, Earl Grey's carrier was starting to feel heavy, but she rolled her shoulders and followed her dad and her trundling suitcase across a busy junction of cars, black taxis, and claret-red and cream double-decker buses.

They entered a street of matching three-story stone buildings with ground floor sandwich shops, small cafes and even the blue-tiled facade of a fishmonger. She caught the tangy scent of the catch of the day and Earl Grey gave a brighter, more hopeful, "Meow."

"Why are there so many tourists in Edinburgh?" asked Dotty, as her father halted and waited for her in front of a square Palladian style building with two stone columns.

"We've been plagued with them all summer. Visiting the castle, attending the festival, and riding around in open-top buses. I know to keep clear of the old town but now they're spilling over into new town and getting in folks' way."

"Where's new town?" asked Dotty.

"This is it. The buildings on this side of the railway, down to the Port of Leith and the sea. The main railway line runs east to west, dividing the city along the base of the old Nor' Loch, a lake created by King James III. Before that it was marshland protecting the approach to Edinburgh Castle, which sits high above it on the volcanic Castle Rock. The area around the castle is old town, and tourists love its narrow, cobbled streets and shops full of tartan, Loch Ness Monster fridge magnets, and toy highland cows."

He pronounced the last word as "coos."

Her dad turned into a quieter residential street lined with terraces of uniform two and three-storey buildings. The once cream stone was tinged with black soot and pollution. A car passed slowly along the uneven square-cobbled road, stopped, and reversed into a free parking space.

"Your mum chose the flat."

That didn't surprise Dotty.

"It's within walking distance of her work and quiet enough, for a city," remarked her dad in an indifferent tone.

"Didn't you want to move?" Dotty hadn't visited them in their last house on the edge of Stirling, a city to the north-west of Edinburgh, but she had seen photos of their newish looking detached house.

"I'm getting used to it," was all her father said as he pushed open a small black iron gate and descended a set of stone steps. A grey door was located in a side wall under what must be the access bridge to the ground-floor flat.

"Your mum promised she wouldn't be late home, but to save you cooking, she's booked us a table at the Mussel Inn on Rose Street. Do you still like seafood?"

It sounded delicious. She'd eaten a lot of meat, fruit, and vegetables in France but little fish.

Passing through the entrance porch, her dad pulled open a door and they entered a light, elegant, open-plan living area with a u-shaped kitchen in front of them and a pair of French windows at the far end.

"Wow," exclaimed Dotty.

"You like it," grunted her father. "Personally, I feel as if I'm living in a hotel room. I daren't put my can of beer down anywhere."

The flat was modern, with stripped and varnished oak floorboards and matching kitchen cupboards. The walls were painted either grey or light blue.

"But you still have your leather chair."

Beyond an oval oak dining table, was her dad's well-used and well-loved, high wing-back leather chair. For as long as she could remember, he'd insisted on moving it from one military quarter to another.

And it seemed that although her mother had exchanged their old pine furniture and stained sofas and armchairs for quality pieces of furniture, she'd allowed the chair to remain.

"Let me show you your room. I guess you'll want to unpack?" suggested her dad, leading her into a tastefully decorated double bedroom with a large sash window looking out of the front of the flat onto a stone wall.

Placing Earl Grey's carrier on the fluffy grey blanket at the end of the bed, which matched her cat's long thick grey coat, she looked out of the window and up at the street as a pair of brown shoes and jean-clad legs passed by.

"Is it OK?" asked her dad from the doorway. He sounded concerned.

She turned to him and smiled. "Of course it's OK. It's lovely."

"Meow."

"I'll let Earl Grey out, but I'll keep the door shut for the moment while he familiarises himself with his new home. And I'd love a cup of tea."

"I'll put the kettle on," said Dotty's dad, sounding relieved to have something to do.

Dotty unzipped the front of the cat carrier and flinched. Although she'd cleaned it out at Newcastle Airport, and put fresh strips of an old towel in, the smell was still overpowering. Conscious of the crisp white waffle-patterned duvet cover, she zipped the carrier back up.

She looked at Earl Grey and said, "Come on. Let's clean you up in the bathroom."

CHAPTER THREE

In the snug ensuite shower room in her parent's Edinburgh flat, Dotty unzipped the front of the black canvas cat carrier.

Earl Grey tentatively poked his head out and sounded a quiet, "Meow."

"I know, boy, it is strange being here. Like coming back to my parents means I've failed in some way."

Dotty knelt on the floor and watched as Earl Grey raised his head and slowly considered the white-tiled walls and painted ceiling.

"You should have seen me as a girl. I wasn't your typical teenager," she said glumly as she scratched her cat's chin. "All I wanted to do was please my dad. To be a model little wife."

"Meow!" Earl Grey retreated into his carrier.

"I'm so sorry." She must have scratched harder than she'd meant to.

Tentatively, Earl Grey peered out, his large yellow eyes considering her warily.

"It was my dad who wanted me to be a model wife, so he could marry me off. And he was so chuffed when he did. If we stay here long enough, he'll tell you how he came from a working-class family and made his way up the ranks to warrant officer, whatever that is."

Earl Grey placed one paw uncertainly on the vinyl floor.

"Captain Alistair Sayers. Dad was so proud when I married a captain, and he told me not to worry that Al was fifteen years older than me. Al would keep me safe. And I guess life was secure. A military house. A military salary. And a military social life."

She stroked Earl Grey's head as he finally emerged from his carrier.

"I did what was expected of me, and I suppose I had a few friends. Other wives who'd moved to a place they didn't know and had no reason to get to know. But that life feels so surreal now. Drifting from one day to the next, cooking, cleaning, and walking Al's black Labrador, Banff."

Earl Grey purred. Using a clean cloth, she wiped each of his paws.

"I've no idea what you'd have thought of him, but he'd have loved you, and so would Al's children from his first marriage." Children she'd done her best to love, but they weren't her own. Al hadn't wanted another family. But that was not a road to go down now.

Using the sink, Dotty pulled herself to her feet and zipped up the carrier. She'd clean it later.

Looking down at Earl Grey, she explained, "And then it all changed. Al went on that peacekeeping tour to Africa, and he died, and never came back." She sat down on the closed toilet lid as Earl Grey rubbed against her legs.

"I don't understand why I don't feel anything when I think about his death. Just a void, a numbness."

Earl Grey rubbed more insistently.

She smiled at him. "You want food, don't you?"

Standing up, she opened the bathroom door and returned to her neat, elegant bedroom. From her green canvas bag, she removed the bag of treats she'd been tempting Earl Grey with during their journey.

Her large fluffy grey cat jumped onto the bed, and she sat down next to him.

"And then I surprised myself and landed a job at Akemans auction house and antiques centre." She opened the bag and placed several pillow-shaped treats on the bed in front of Earl Grey. He crunched them greedily.

"And it's been fun working there, finding you, and moving into our little cottage at Meadowbank Farm."

Earl Grey looked up at her and she rubbed his chin again. "Do you miss Aunt Beanie feeding you titbits?"

In response, he butted her leg. She got out some more treats.

"Aunt Beanie feels like family to me, but she isn't really, and Akemans? Looking back at my first few days, not long after burying Al, I can't believe I stayed. Not when I actually had to talk to people." She smiled to herself. "But it was fun, and learning about antiques has been a challenge."

Having devoured his treats, Earl Grey stared at the packet she was still holding.

"I think you've had enough. And perhaps I've had enough of Akemans. The auctions and stalls in the antiques centre are fun and interesting, but the counterfeit furniture, stolen and forged paintings, and so many deaths. I can't believe I didn't realise what was happening."

She lifted her hand to her throat. The red marks had faded, and the French sun had tanned her skin, hiding them, but she could still feel her scarf being pulled tightly around her neck. And by a man she'd trusted. Who she'd considered her mentor.

Pushing herself to her feet, she said, "You better stay in here for now, but I'll bring you some proper food."

Closing the door of the guest bedroom, she heard a soft, "meow". Earl Grey continued to complain and scratch the door as she opened a sachet of meaty cat food, tipping it into the new porcelain bowl with a picture of a fish skeleton on the side which her mother had bought specially.

"OK, OK," she relented, opening her bedroom door. "I don't want to be trapped here either."

CHAPTER FOUR

Dotty sat back in a wrought iron chair watching Earl Grey explore the ivy-clad stone wall which separated her parent's small patio terrace from the garden of the neighbouring building.

"This is nice," she told her father politely as he placed a white mug, decorated with a blue and yellow floral pattern, on the wrought iron table.

"We're very lucky," he replied, setting his own cup of coffee on the table as he sat down.

"Gardens are communal for tenement flats, but the previous owners of our flat did a deal with the other owners in the building, which allowed them to create a small private terrace in return for maintaining the remaining garden." He inclined his head to a lower level of flagstones. "Luckily, the owners also agreed to pave over the grass, so there isn't too much work for me to do."

Dotty considered the view of the rear of the buildings on the parallel street, and suspected the terrace would be shaded from the early morning sun, whose soft rays were now warming her as the earlier clouds had almost all departed.

"You mentioned a festival earlier. That sounds fun. What's it about?" enquired Dotty as she lifted her mug. She savoured the floral tones of Earl Grey tea.

"I know little about the international one. It's a bit highbrow for me. Concerts and lavish theatre productions, that sort of thing."

"Oh." Her father's response disappointed Dotty.

Her dad gave her a lopsided smile. "But there's also the Fringe Festival. Your mum and I used to leave you with a babysitter and spend an afternoon and evening in small, cramped rooms in the Seven Sisters pub, or the big top tent on the Meadows. We'd watch fresh-faced comedians, innovative new acts, and some really bizarre performances. We once took you to a puppet show. Do you remember?"

Dotty shook her head.

"But your mum went with work last year and she said it's really busy, even during preview week."

"What's preview week?"

Dotty sipped her tea, as her father responded, "It's the week I prefer, the first week of the festival when you can get half price or even free entry to shows. Performers want audiences so the people who attend will spread the word and hopefully provide publicity for their shows."

"Can we do that?" asked Dotty enthusiastically.

"It's nearly over but ask your mum. She's going to watch a comedian with some work mates tomorrow night."

Dotty made lunch for herself and her father from the meagre supplies in the flat. Tinned soup with a mixture of sliced ham and Ardennes pâté sandwiches. There didn't appear to be a single vegetable in the flat.

"Thanks," muttered her dad, as he picked up his bowl of soup. "Your mum suggested I take you to the supermarket this afternoon, as you'd be appalled by the contents of our fridge and our current eating habits."

"Which are?" asked Dotty, carrying her bowl and plate out to the stone terrace.

Her dad followed her as he replied, "Cafes, takeaways, and ready meals. As you know, your mum doesn't eat much, so she's never seen the point of cooking. I fend for myself, and often start the day with brunch at a local cafe on Broughton Street, which means I don't need anything else until supper. But this makes a pleasant change," he said as he placed his bowl on the wrought iron outdoor table.

Earl Grey joined them, rubbing against Dotty's legs. "Are you feeling better?" asked Dotty, tearing off a strip of ham from inside her sandwich and dropping it onto a flagstone.

Earl Grey pounced on it greedily.

At half-past six, Dotty emerged from her ensuite bathroom, steam following her out. With a large fluffy white towel wrapped round her body, and a smaller one round her head, she heard her father call, "Your mum's running late. She said she'd meet us at the restaurant."

Through the closed bedroom door, Dotty heard the muffled sounds of a rugby or football match her father was watching on the large flat screen TV. He'd sat down in his leather chair with a cold beer as soon as they'd returned from food shopping, leaving Dotty to unpack.

Dotty unwrapped the towel from around her head and shook her bobbed, highlighted blonde hair, bleached even fairer by the French sun. She'd let it grow out while she was away, and she knew her mum would immediately recommend a salon where she could have it cut and restyled. She needed to, but sometimes she wished her mum would look beyond her outward appearance.

Maybe that's why, until recently, she hadn't cared how she looked. Her mother was fastidious about remaining thin. And she was always following one health fad or another. But she'd always exercised, finding a local fitness group wherever they were posted. Maybe that was how she found her friends.

It must have been hard for her mum, moving around the country. Dotty had only moved house once while she was married, but as a child, it seemed that they were forever on the move. She'd certainly attended more schools than she cared to remember.

"We'll leave in ten minutes," called her dad through the closed door.

As Dotty surveyed a choice of clothes on her bed - the ditsy floral brown and cream dress with buttons down the front, or the red and green floral print, wide legged trousers - she realised she was nervous about meeting her mother again. How long had it been since she'd seen her? Five years?

She chose the trousers. Although the sun had shone all afternoon, she wasn't sure how warm the Edinburgh evening would be.

Five years since she and her mum had met in person, with only brief, polite phone conversations at Christmas and on her birthday in those years. Would she be able to reconnect with the woman who'd never really been a mother to her?

CHAPTER FIVE

The Edinburgh evening was warmer than Dotty had expected. She felt a bead of perspiration on her forehead as she and her father strode along Rose Street, a narrow lane running parallel to the much wider and commercial Princes Street, and the far grander George Street.

It was twenty past seven and chattering people packed their route, meandering about, or standing and consulting mobile phones. And they were from all nationalities. Dotty listened to the mixture of foreign phrases and accents.

She'd thought the Cotswolds attracted a lot of visitors, but Edinburgh was on a whole different level.

"See what I mean?" muttered her father. "Why can't these tourists stick to the Royal Mile?"

"Royal Mile?" enquired Dotty.

They emerged from their current section of Rose Street, needing to cross the wider road in front of them, which connected George Street and Princes Street. She'd already learned that in this section of the city, the wide streets were arranged in a grid pattern with two squares, St Andrew's and Charlotte, at either end.

"Come this way." Instead of crossing the road, her dad turned left and joined the flow of pedestrians. They stopped before they reached

Princes Street, beside a gentleman's outfitters displaying brown tweed trousers and jackets in the shop window.

Opposite them, Dotty saw an imposing stone building with columns supporting an ornate carved roof on which she could see the statue of an imperial looking woman, she recognised as Queen Victoria.

"That's the Royal Academy," remarked her dad, following her gaze. "It, and the National Gallery of Scotland behind it, are art galleries. I think they're free to enter. But what I wanted to show you is the castle." His arm pointed diagonally across Princes Street and Dotty gasped.

In the distance, rising high above the trees, was a collection of stone buildings on a rocky outcrop, surround by a tall stone wall.

"It's not a typical castle, it looks more like a small village," declared Dotty.

"I suppose it is. And it's worth visiting, although I'm not sure that's possible at the moment with the Tattoo."

"Tattoo?" Dotty asked, confused by yet another unknown Edinburgh phrase.

"Now that I would like to take you to. I took part one year, when there were more soldiers, and it was less commercialised."

"But what is it?"

"A performance, or display, of marching military bands, Scottish dancers and other acts. These days there are also lots of foreign performers, but it's still worth seeing. If you're interested, I'll try to get us some tickets. If there are any left."

Still feeling slightly overwhelmed, but delighted about her father's enthusiasm to do something with her, she asked, "And the Royal Mile?"

"Ah, yes. It runs from the esplanade outside the castle, where the stage and seating for the Tattoo are set up, downhill to Holyrood Palace. The royal family still uses the palace, and it's the King's official residence in Scotland. That's somewhere else you could visit, but again, it'll be busy."

As they crossed the road, consumed by a mass of other people, Dotty resigned herself to everywhere being busy in Edinburgh during her stay.

They approached a restaurant whose ice-blue chairs and square wooden tables occupied half the narrow street, so pedestrians had to squeeze between them and the building opposite.

"I hope your mum booked a table inside, away from all these people," complained her dad, as they joined a queue to enter the restaurant space.

A hand waved at them through a window.

"Good, there she is," declared Dotty's dad, and he pushed past the waiting diners and entered the restaurant.

Dotty's mum, who had always preferred to be called by her Christian name, Karen, stood up behind the table she'd secured beside the window.

Dotty felt Karen's appraising eyes as she squeezed between tables of chatting diners. They didn't hug or embrace but politely air kissed each other.

"You look good," approved Karen. "Although your hair needs restyling. I'll organise an appointment for you at Cheynes on George Street."

"You found her then?" Karen directed her question at Dotty's dad.

"All sorted and the cat hasn't escaped yet, and I took Dotty to the supermarket this afternoon, so we've restocked the cupboards and fridge."

"Excellent," declared Karen, picking up a menu. She didn't enquire about Dotty's health, her journey, or offer any similar small talk. Not even an apology for meeting them at the restaurant instead of at the flat. And she was straight down to business.

"As it's your first time here, I recommend one of the kilo pots of mussels," directed Karen.

A smiling waiter appeared behind Dotty's dad and said, "Drinks?"

Karen downed the remnants of her current drink, handed the highball glass to the waiter and stated, "A bottle of white, whichever you recommend goes best with scallops."

"Beer, for me," requested her dad.

"And can I have a glass of tap water?" asked Dotty.

Karen peered at her over her glasses with a 'do you have to ask for that?' stare.

"Ice and lemon?" checked the waiter.

Dotty nodded.

Karen moved her head to stare out of the window and instinctively, Dotty knew this was her cue to choose what to eat.

The kilo pots of mussels looked interesting, and she presumed that from the restaurant's name that they were the house speciality. But she couldn't decide between the shallot, with white wine, garlic and cream, and the blue cheese with bacon and cream.

The waiter returned with their drinks, uncorking the bottle of wine, and pouring a sample into Karen's glass. Her mother sipped and swirled the liquid around her mouth before swallowing. She nodded at the waiter, who filled hers and Dotty's glasses. He rested the bottle in a chrome stand he'd placed beside their table.

Dotty decided to stick to the classic shallot mussels, with a side order of French fries which she knew would annoy her mother.

The waiter returned with her dad's beer and her water and, when he'd placed them on the table, he asked, "Are you ready to order?"

"The king scallops," Karen said, without consulting the menu. She picked up her glass and sipped her wine.

The waiter moved his attention to Dotty.

"The shallot mussels," she requested.

"Half or a full kilo?"

Dotty hesitated.

"She'll have the full kilo," rescued her dad, "and a side order of French fries."

Karen tutted but Dotty smiled gratefully at her father.

"And I'll have the sea bass as my main and for a starter, to share, the haggis bonbons."

Karen pressed her lips together in disapproval, but Dotty's dad said, "When in Scotland."

Dotty had eaten haggis before at regimental Burn's Night dinners to commemorate the Scottish poet, but those had been some time ago.

When the waiter left, Karen said, "I can take a few days off work, but we're starting a new advertising campaign in September, which still needs pulling together. Is there anything in particular you want to do or see?"

Dotty refrained from replying that she'd really come to see her mum and dad and spend time with them. Instead she muttered, "There seem to be so many things. I'm not sure where to start."

"Euan," Karen said to Dotty's dad, "Why don't you show Dotty around tomorrow so she can orientate herself. I'm taking my work team to see a comedian at the Pleasance in the evening but you're welcome to join us for supper afterwards."

Karen turned her attention to Dotty. "You might enjoy soaking up the atmosphere in the Pleasance Courtyard. There's always something going on. And plenty of food," Karen paused and looked at Euan, "and drink stalls."

The waiter placed a bowl of crispy breadcrumb-coated balls on the table and, beside it, a smaller bowl containing a deep-red dip. Karen broke off a piece of the accompanying parmesan crisp as Dotty picked up a haggis bonbon and dunked it in the roasted red pepper dip.

Delicious.

CHAPTER SIX

"Morning," mumbled Dotty the following day, as she opened her bedroom door and saw her father leaning over a bowl of cereal. He was sitting at a small, circular wooden table positioned at the junction of the kitchen and living room spaces.

"Ah, Dotty. Good to see you up," announced Karen as she entered the kitchen from the entrance hall. She placed a brown envelope on the table next to Euan and sorted through the remaining post.

"Excellent, there's a Fringe Festival programme here which you can look through and see if there's anything you'd like to see." She placed a brightly coloured booklet on the table and pushed it towards Dotty. "And these are …" Karen paused. "That's a shame, they're addressed to someone else but you two could still go."

"Go where?" muttered Euan.

"To the opening night of *Underground Murder*, a play being performed by The Spa Players from Cheltenham."

Dotty blinked at Karen, her interest piqued. She knew the Victorian spa town of Cheltenham and had often visited when she'd lived in the Cotswolds.

"And why would we want to go?" persisted Euan.

"Because we've been sent two VIP tickets and you, being a Scotsman, never turn down something that's free."

"True enough," he mumbled, returning to his bowl of cereal.

"May I have a look?" asked Dotty, holding out her hand.

Karen passed the invitations over and tucked the remaining envelope in the side of her canvas briefcase. "And I must leave for work. That play's in the Pleasance Side Theatre, so whether you go or not, why not join me and my team in the Pleasance Courtyard at half-past five?"

"We'll see," grunted Euan.

"OK," replied Dotty, smiling. It was likely to be the closest she'd get to an invitation from her mother.

At a quarter to six, a puffing Dotty arrived at a collection of Edinburgh University buildings with a bright yellow banner running down the stone face of one, with 'The Pleasance' printed on it. As well as being busy, Edinburgh was hilly.

Her dad, red in the face, joined her and they entered the complex through a stone archway. Inside, another yellow banner hanging from one of the gable-fronted, three-storey stone buildings which enclosed the area, announced they were in 'The Courtyard'.

Smiling young people, probably university students earning some holiday money before the start of a new academic year, were handing out colourful flyers. Politely Dotty accepted flyers for plays, acrobatic performances, and stand-up comedians.

The atmosphere was fun and full of excited anticipation. An old-fashioned red telephone box stood in the corner. As she passed it, a man wearing three-quarter length trousers and a bow tie asked, "Would you like to join our world record-breaking attempt to fit the most people into a telephone box?"

Dotty shied away from the man and his phone box. There was no way she was getting crushed inside it.

"What's the existing record?" asked her father, halting beside the eccentric-looking man.

"We set it at fourteen last year."

"Fourteen! I think that's quite enough," and Euan shook his head as he re-joined Dotty and remarked, "What some people will do for fame."

They found Karen with a group of men and women, mostly younger than her, sitting at a couple of wooden picnic tables in the cobbled Pleasance courtyard.

Around the perimeter of the courtyard, under bright yellow canopies, there were bars and drinks kiosks, and a variety of food stalls selling such delicacies as falafel, Hawaiian Poke bowls, and award-winning ice cream.

"You made it," acknowledged Karen, looking up and halting her conversation with the young man next to her, as Dotty and her father stopped beside the tables. "You'll probably want a beer, Euan, but we've a jug of mojito on the go if you'd like some, Dotty."

Karen didn't introduce Dotty to the group but restarted her conversation with the young man.

Euan disappeared into the crowd and, for a moment, Dotty was frozen to the spot, not sure what to do next.

"Dotty, isn't it? Why don't you try a glass of this? It looks like you need to cool down." The only woman who looked similar in age to Karen smiled and held up a clear plastic glass with leaves of fresh mint floating in it.

Dotty stepped forward as a girl younger than her shuffled along the bench, making room for Dotty to sit down opposite the pleasant, motherly looking woman.

"I'm Gail," said the woman, handing Dotty the glass. "I make sure the team keep functioning and go home at night. Honestly, if I didn't, I think half of them would sleep at the office."

The girl next to Dotty leaned closer and whispered, "I did two weeks ago when the last train home was cancelled."

Gail pressed her lips together, but she gave the girl a sympathetic rather than disapproving look. "You mum's been so excited about your visit," Gail revealed.

"She has?" blurted Dotty, her tone disbelieving.

"Don't be put off by her direct, often abrupt manner. It's how she's done so well for herself at the bank." Gail leaned forward and confided, "It's a bit of an old boys' club." She sat up.

"But she is delighted you're visiting, and I'd actually say it's the first time I've seen her nervous. That's why she couldn't meet you off the train. Made up an excuse about having a meeting."

Dotty frowned in confusion. Her mother was nervous about meeting her?

"Anyway, you're here now, which is great. Just make sure you spend some quality time with your mum. Take her to an art gallery. I think that's your kind of thing. Or get away from the crowds with a long walk along Portobello beach."

Dotty nodded uncertainly, unable to imagine an intimate beach walk or discussing modern art with Karen.

"And what have you done today?" Gail asked.

This was easier territory for Dotty. "My dad showed me round the new town this morning, and we walked here this afternoon via the Royal Mile. I can't believe Edinburgh is so hilly, though!"

"Personally, I avoid the walk up The Mound from Princes Street," admitted Gail. "And the Royal Mile is unbearable at this time of year. You should come back in the Autumn or Spring to fully appreciate it."

"Are you going to the play?" Karen called across.

"Which play is that?" asked Gail in a curious tone.

Dotty pulled the two VIP invitations out of her bag and handed them across.

"Who are Simon Everett and Scarlet Jones?" asked Gail. They were the handwritten names at the top of the invitations.

"Dad said they were the previous occupants of his and Karen's flat. He thinks one of them was a journalist."

"So the invites are actually for them. How exciting. You must go and see what it's all about," insisted Gail.

"But I can't use someone else's invitation," protested Dotty.

"Of course, you can. It happens all the time during the festival as people swap tickets and shows."

Dotty thought exchanging tickets was not the same as gate-crashing an event, pretending to be someone else.

In the silence that fell between Dotty and Gail, the older woman looked round and, catching someone's eye, waved.

"Let me introduce you to Morag," said Gail, still looking over Dotty's shoulder.

A woman in her early fifties joined them, standing at the end of the picnic table. Her eyes continued to roam the milling crowd, and she looked uncomfortable, squeezed into a denim jacket and jogging bottoms.

"Are you off duty?" asked Gail, a note of surprise in her voice.

"No, but they insisted we wear plain clothes to mingle with the crowd." She sounded as uncomfortable as she looked.

"Ooh, undercover work. So now we have an undercover policewoman and someone else's invitation to a mysterious event." Gail was clearly caught up in the drama of the Fringe Festival.

Morag glanced up at the blue sky with thin strands of cloud and shook her head. Then she said, in a disgruntled tone, "I'm not undercover, and what invitation are you talking about?"

Gail picked up one of the invites Dotty had left on the table and handed it to Morag, whose eyes widened. "And are you Scarlet Jones?"

Gail laughed. "This is Karen's daughter, Dotty, and she could be useful to you. She's an amateur detective."

Dotty's mouth opened and closed. She felt like an idiot. What would this down-to-earth looking Scottish policewoman think of her, and anyway, how did Gail know that she'd been helping Gloucestershire police force?

"Are you now?" replied Morag dubiously. "Well, perhaps you can help me find whoever keeps dressing the statue of Blackfriars Bobby in Celtic football kit."

Dotty's embarrassment turned to bewilderment.

Gail smiled. "Ask your father to explain that."

Morag was staring at the invitation, her lips pressed together. In a solemn tone, she asked, "Have you really helped the police?"

"I have friends in one of the serious crimes squads at Cirencester police station, and we've worked together on a number of cases."

"And solved them," Gail said, nodding her head with a knowing looking on her face.

But how did she know?

Morag placed her hands on the table and, leaning closer to them, whispered, "Then you might be able to help me out." She tapped the invitation. "This is the event I'm here for. Some important people have been invited to the opening night and there are concerns for their safety."

Gail's eyes widened. "What type of important people?"

Morag fixed her with a stare and said, "Let's just say one of them has been causing waves lately in the Scottish Parliament."

"Oh, I see. Mum's the word." Gail closed her mouth and raised a finger to it. But then she brightened and asked, "What do you want Dotty to do?"

"Those with VIP tickets will be seated at the front of the theatre and then asked to take part in the play."

Dotty sat back and protested, "I'm not being part of any play."

"Don't worry," soothed Morag. "You don't have to say anything. Just stand as if you're on a train and react to the drama as it unfolds. I'll be in the theatre, but I'd feel much happier having someone keeping a lookout on the stage."

"A lookout for what?" queried Dotty.

Morag lowered her voice and whispered. "Iona McDuff is the person of interest, and she has strong views on Scottish independence, which not everyone agrees with. Recently, she's been receiving more than her usual level of hate mail."

"Didn't your boss, Assistant Chief Constable Rhona Cameron, suggest she stay away?" asked Gail.

"She did, but there's a family connection with this play. Apparently, it was first performed at the festival twenty-five years ago by the same theatre group. The leader at the time, Willoughby Thorpe ..."

"I've heard of him," interjected Gail.

"That's because he's now a vocal member of the House of Lords and has taken up the cause to keep Scotland in the United Kingdom."

"So what has he got to do with Iona McDuff?" asked Gail.

Dotty was just about managing to keep up with the conversation.

"Ms McDuff's mother is a friend of Lord Thorpe's wife, Suzie. But Suzie very ill. In fact, I'm not sure she's actually travelled with him. Even so, Iona McDuff has been invited to opening night."

"Isn't this exciting?" Gail looked across at Dotty. "You'll have to go now. Remind me, what's the play called?"

Morag replied thinly, "*Underground Murder*."

CHAPTER SEVEN

"Time we found our seats," Karen announced, standing up.

Morag, the undercover policewoman, straightened up and looked around the Pleasance's bustling courtyard. "I better go too, and so should you," she instructed Dotty.

"I really don't know," Dotty protested.

"Oh, go on. What else are you going to do?" asked her mother's team member, Gail. "Watch the play, enjoy yourself, and meet us for supper afterwards."

"Come on," insisted Karen, looking at Gail.

Gail climbed over the back of the bench. She gave Dotty an encouraging smile as she left, following Karen towards what in Dotty's mind resembled a graffiti covered totem pole with yellow arms extending in many directions, each with the large image of an over-sized finger and a name which Dotty presumed was a venue.

Euan joined Dotty, standing beside her table. "What do you think? Do you want to watch a performance or head back to the flat?"

"Well …" What did she want to do? The sensible side of her mind told her she'd had an interesting day and should return to the flat.

But another side, which had become more insistent since Al had died and she'd started to act independently, urged 'come on girl, you have to try this. You're in Edinburgh with so many exciting things going on. You can't hide away in your parent's flat.'

"While we're here, and we do have free entry, perhaps we should watch this play. And if it's no good, we can just get up and leave," she suggested.

"I suppose so," replied her dad hesitantly.

"And someone called Iona McDuff has also been invited to watch it."

"Has she? Then it can't be that bad."

The attendance of the Scottish MP seemed to have swayed her father.

"Which venue?" he asked.

Dotty glanced at the tickets. "Pleasance Side Theatre."

Various groups of people were snaking towards different venues, and they followed one of the lines to a building with 'Side' printed on a yellow banner hanging on the wall.

Inside, the theatre was modest, with no more than a dozen rows of seats facing a raised stage. The building itself had curved wooden ceiling beams and it was very atmospheric.

The usher at the entrance, whom Dotty presumed was another student, read their invitations and signalled to a flush-faced young woman in her early to mid-twenties. "Two more VIPs," muttered the usher as the young woman approached.

She took a deep breath and arranged her face into a welcoming smile. "I'm Skye, the show's assistant producer, and we're all delighted you could join us this evening. Please follow me." She wore a polka dot skirt with a bandana around her neck, and she'd tied her long hair back in a ponytail.

"She looks as if she's stepped out of the 1950s," Euan commented to Dotty as he followed her and Skye down the left-hand side of the theatre. As they approached the front, Dotty noticed a raised platform to the left of the stage, housing banks of controls for the technical aspects of the performance.

Skye stopped at the end of the second row from the front, which contained eight seats, and explained, "As this is the opening of the 25th anniversary of the show, we'd like you to celebrate with us and participate, albeit with silent roles. These are your places."

She pointed to the two unoccupied seats at the end of the row. On one seat, there was a bowler hat and propped against it a black briefcase and a closed black umbrella. Resting on the other seat, there was a grey wig with a bun, a pair of black-rimmed glasses, and a shopping basket containing a vintage cereal box and a brown paper bag full of apples.

"What are we supposed to do?" asked Euan, uncertainly.

Skye replied, "Dressed as ordinary people from 1950s London, you'll follow the other VIPs along your row and onto the stage. As you'll be the last on, find a space, either on a seat in the carriage or standing by one of the rails or hanging straps marked with a luminous yellow sticker. Then watch the action unfurl and react as any passenger would, faced with such a situation. Feel free to gasp, or cry out, but please don't swear. This is a family show."

Even though it involved a murder, thought Dotty.

"Will you excuse me?" Skye left them and returned to the entrance where Dotty saw Morag entering the theatre. They locked eyes, but Morag didn't acknowledge her.

"I didn't realise performing on stage was the price of our free invites. Do you think it would be rude to leave now?" asked Euan.

Dotty glanced along the row. There was a young woman with curly auburn hair poking out from under a headscarf and a copper-skinned lady with large white glasses and a matching white handbag on her lap. Her partner wore a trilby and carried a cane and the man next to him wore a flat cap and held a rolled-up newspaper.

They all looked apprehensive, tugging at their clothes, fidgeting, or speaking earnestly to their neighbours.

Dotty realised she wasn't the only nervous one. She looked back at the rapidly filling auditorium and then at the stage and felt a twinge of excitement. But what an opportunity. Not everyone could say they'd performed in front of an audience at the Edinburgh Fringe Festival.

"I think we should sit down and go with flow," said Dotty. "Besides, I've heard that once you're on stage, with all the lights and such, you can't even see the audience."

Her dad frowned but turned and picked up the bowler hat, positioning it on the back of his head.

Dotty giggled. "Here, let me help." She repositioned his hat, so it sat comfortably on his head, and then she picked up the basket and placed it at the end of the row so she could sit down. As she tucked strands of her own hair under the grey wig, she hoped she wouldn't forget the basket.

A hush fell in the auditorium and Skye returned escorting a haughty-looking woman in her early forties who wore a striking blue and green knee-length tartan dress with a full swing skirt and a small, elegant, ivory-coloured crescent hat on the side of her head.

Dotty wrinkled her brow. Clearly, someone had briefed this lady about her role and she had come dressed for the part.

"That's Iona McDuff, the MSP," whispered her dad.

Iona took her place in the centre of the front row, and Skye climbed onto the control platform beside the stage and started tapping switches and turning dials. The lights in the theatre dimmed as rock 'n' roll music started to play. The audience fell silent.

CHAPTER EIGHT

The lights lit up a structure on the centre of the stage which resembled the interior of a London Underground tube carriage. Dotty presumed the gaps at either end were supposed to be the doors and inside there were two sets of seats with brown and blue mottled covers.

A rail began by the door and wrapped around the rear perimeter of the makeshift carriage at head height. Several nylon straps hung from it.

The rock 'n' roll music was replaced by the noise of a train and the screeching of brakes symbolising its slowing to a stop. A disembodied voice announced, "This is Earl's Court. Change here for the Piccadilly line."

A man carrying a newspaper and briefcase, dressed in a pinstripe suit, and wearing a bowler hat identical to the one Dotty's father was wearing, entered the stage from the left.

On the right, a younger man also stepped onto the stage wearing a white t-shirt under a black leather jacket. He'd slicked his hair into a pompadour style like Elvis Presley.

There was a swooshing noise, to represent the doors opening, and both men entered the carriage, sitting down opposite each other on the left-hand pair of seats. The man in the pinstripe suit opened his newspaper and ignored his companion.

The lights dimmed and train noises sounded again until there was a screeching of brakes and this time a voice called, "South Kensington. Change here for the Piccadilly and Circle Lines."

This time a man wearing a flat tweed cap, baggy trousers, and a wool jumper with several holes in it, joined the train and sat in the second set of seats, his back to the young man with the black leather jacket.

The imaginary train moved on again, and in the darkness, they heard a voice ask, "Do you take this route every day, gov?"

The stage lights brightened slightly, but the train noise continued. Skye left her control booth and indicated to the copper-skinned lady, with the white glasses and handbag, who stood up and pushed past other people in her row. Skye whispered to her, and she climbed onto the stage to stand beside the train doors on the right of the carriage.

Then Skye indicated that the remaining guests in the second row should stand. They did so, and filed onto the stage, queuing for the train behind the lady with the white hat.

Dotty tapped her father's elbow, and he hesitantly stood up. Dotty's heart thumped as she shuffled along the row and followed the other VIP guests up onto the stage. As she did, the front row, led by Iona McDuff, took the stairs by the control booth, and queued beside the imaginary train doors on the left of the stage.

Skye returned to her control booth and the noise of the moving train, which had continued while the VIP guests took their positions, quietened and, with a screeching of brakes, the disembodied voice announced, "London Victoria. Change here for the Circle and Victoria lines, and for overland trains from London Victoria."

After the noise of the doors opening, the VIP guests filed in. The lady with the white glasses sat on a seat at the end of the row nearest the door. Her partner sat opposite her, next to the actor with the tweed cap, and another lady pushed passed them and sat down on the fourth seat, so that all the places were occupied.

Nobody sat down on the other seats but stood around the perimeter, holding one of the hanging nylon straps. The makeshift carriage looked rather full when Dotty and her father stepped in, but there was a space next to Iona McDuff.

Dotty felt her father hesitate, so she whispered, "This is your chance to stand next to the MP."

"MSP," whispered her father, but he pushed past other guests and took his place beside Iona, holding onto the free nylon strap.

The young man in the leather jacket started speaking and, panicking, Dotty noticed a luminous yellow strip of tape on the metal bar next to her, which supported the overhead rail. Breathing out in relief, she grabbed hold of it as the man in the pinstripe suit replied. Dotty, her nerves calming, finally tuned into the conversation.

"I live alone during the week," said the man in the pinstripe suit.

The lights dimmed and the train noise started again, but suddenly a woman cried out in panic, "I don't like this!"

In the darkness, Dotty heard shuffling and felt the other guests tense, unsure what was happening.

"Bang!"

A gun. People screamed.

Dotty jumped and then grabbed the rail even harder. She felt movement near her but couldn't see anything. Her eyes hadn't adjusted to the dark after the bright stage lights.

"Bang." A muffled noise this time and someone pushed past her.

She waited in silence, expecting something to happen.

Someone whispered, "Where are the lights?"

The noise of brakes and, as the disembodied voice announced, "This is Westminster," the audience gasped.

Dotty blinked several times in the glare of the bright lights. And then she saw the lady with the white hat slumped back against her seat. A bright red patch on her chest.

It was very realistic, thought Dotty as she noticed the lady's chest rise and fall. She was just acting.

Then someone cried, "Iona McDuff. She's dead!

CHAPTER NINE

Dotty stood on the stage in the Pleasance Side Theatre and locked eyes with her dad.

His face was pale, even in the harsh stage lighting, and his eyes wide and fearful.

She wanted to comfort him, but she was rooted to the spot. Her eyes moved to the empty nylon strap beside him where the Member of the Scottish Parliament, Iona McDuff, had been standing, and down to her father's feet. But nobody was there.

The man in the pinstripe suit stood up at the far end of the left-hand row of seats and looked down at a figure, who was slumped forward. Blood splattered her ivory crescent-shaped hat.

"Nobody move," shouted a chubby woman as she ran, rather ungainly, from the back of the theatre towards the stage. She stopped when she reached it and called up, "Police," before gasping for air. It was Morag, the undercover policewoman who looked out of place now in her denim jacket and jogging bottoms.

A policewoman stepped onto the stage from the wings at the back and asked in a clear voice, with the twang of a regional accent Dotty couldn't place, "Did someone call for the police?"

Clearly the other VIP guests on the stage were as confused as Dotty as their eyes darted from Morag to the unknown policewoman.

What was going on? wondered Dotty. Was this real, or part of the performance?

Morag pulled a black wallet out of her jacket pocket, opened it, and held it up towards the stage. "PC Morag Elliot of Police Scotland. Someone shouted that Iona McDuff is dead."

The man in the pinstripe suit turned towards the front of the stage. He had a confident manner and a strong, but rather lined face. His accent was pure British aristocracy, and he said clearly, but regretfully, "I am afraid she is." He turned towards the uniformed policewoman and said, "This is for real, Jenny, not part of the show."

The lady with the white hat abruptly sat up. "You mean someone else is dead? I thought that was my part?"

The guests on stage all started talking at once, as did those in the main theatre.

"Quiet, please," called Morag.

At first, nobody took any notice, but a hush fell as a black uniformed figure strode purposefully down the aisle of the theatre. In her left hand she clasped a black cap, with a black and white checkerboard band, and her hair was pulled back in a severe bun.

A young man in a grey suit ran to catch up with her.

Morag muttered something under her breath, which Dotty was unable to catch.

The newcomer drove straight to the point. "You radioed in for assistance, Constable."

"Yes, Ma'am," replied Morag. She gulped before continuing, "I'm trying to establish if Iona McDuff is dead, while making sure nobody else moves."

"Iona," called the newcomer, in an authoritative voice.

The man in the pinstripe suit stepped into the limited space between the makeshift carriage seats and replied in an equally self-assured manner. "Miss McDuff is here. But she can't respond. She's been shot."

The audience gasped.

Did they know this was real, or like Dotty, were reality and the play blending together for them?

Perhaps the newcomer had the same impression as she turned to the audience and announced, "I am Assistant Chief Constable Rhona

Cameron. I am not a member of the cast and until we have established exactly what has happened, please remain in your seats. This is not part of the performance."

The gravity of her tone when she spoke the last sentence settled on the audience whose members glanced at each other, frowned, or whispered to their neighbours.

Someone on stage whispered, "That's the real ACC, and she's not joking." Those close to Dotty stared across at the slumped figure of Iona McDuff.

A man from the audience approached the ACC, and they held a brief, whispered conversation. He must have been a doctor.

"Accompany Dr Brown onto stage, Constable," the ACC instructed Morag.

Dotty watched as Morag and the doctor climbed onto the stage beside the steps which led to the control booth. Skye was still on the raised platform, her face ashen, and Dotty thought she was crying. Whether for the victim, or the play being ruined on opening night, she wasn't sure.

The doctor knelt by the body and placed his hand against Iona's wrist. After a minute, he stood up and shook his head at the ACC. "She's definitely dead. I better not interfere anymore. You need to notify the procurator fiscal."

The ACC held a whispered conversation with Morag and the young, suited assistant. Then Morag stood in front of the stage and took photographs with her phone.

The ACC strode back towards the theatre entrance.

"I need to sit down," groaned one guest on the stage.

Morag replied, in a kind tone, "Give me a few minutes to photograph you all, and make a sketch, so I'll know where each of you was when the event occurred, and then you can return to your seats. I'm afraid someone will need to interview you before you can leave. It's going to be a long night," she sighed.

Dotty felt as if she was part of a bizarre fashion shoot as Morag took her photo from several different angles, and then took panoramic shots of the whole makeshift carriage, and close-ups of parts of it. She felt trapped within an invisible prison.

Finally, Morag said, "Thank you for your patience," and she

indicated for Dotty to join her. As the other VIP guests filed past and off the stage, Morag whispered, "Did you see who killed the MSP? I was stuck by the theatre entrance and couldn't see anything."

"I'm sorry. When the lights went off, I was in the dark. I did hear someone say they didn't like it and I presumed they meant the darkness. To be honest, everyone was rather tense, so when the first shot rang out it was a shock."

"First shot?" queried Morag. "I only heard one, but do you think there was a second?"

"Yes, it was muffled, but I'm sure there was another. Besides, someone had to pretend to shoot the woman near me, with the white hat and handbag. She's over there." Dotty pointed to the lady who had a red smear across her chest. "She must have been the play's intended victim."

"So which shot killed her?" asked Morag.

Dotty drew her lips together and her shoulders sagged. "Sorry, I've no idea. The darkness and the people. But I did think someone pushed past me after the second shot."

"The killer?" Morag sounded hopeful.

"Dotty, are you all right?" gasped her father as he joined them. He was paler than Dotty had realised.

"I am, but you need to sit down." Dotty helped her father down the steps at the side of the stage and to a vacant theatre chair. "And you need some water." As he sat down, she searched around and found an unopened plastic water bottle wedged under the adjacent seat. She unscrewed the cap and passed it to her father, who slowly sipped from it.

Dotty glanced up at the stage as Morag circled around the makeshift carriage.

"Constable," called the authoritative ACC.

Morag left the stage and joined a group of new arrivals, who included a man and woman wearing plain clothes, and several figures clad in white space suits. The crime scene investigators, thought Dotty.

Her phone vibrated in her pocket.

"Have you finished?" asked Karen curtly. "There are police swarming about everywhere and a couple of television vans have just turned up. I've no idea what's going on, but we're getting out of here. Shall we meet you at The Purple Plum for supper?"

"I'm not sure." Dotty hesitated. What was she allowed to tell Karen? She glanced around and realised most of the audience were also on their phones. The story of Iona McDuff's death was already out there.

"We can't leave at the moment. There's been a murder."

CHAPTER TEN

"Here you are," murmured Karen.

Dotty slowly ran her hand across her left eye removing the gummy substance which seemed to have stuck her eyelids together. Gradually opening both eyes, she looked straight into Karen's smiling, sympathetic face.

"I thought you'd want a lie in after all the drama last night, but it's nearly nine o'clock." Karen placed a mug of milky tea on the bedside table. Gratefully, Dotty pushed herself into a sitting position before reaching for the mug.

"And I'm sorry for pushing you to see the show. Witnessing a murder isn't what I wanted for the start of your visit. How are you feeling?" asked Karen.

"Emotionally drained," Dotty replied. She had witnessed the aftermath of murders before, but to be in such close proximity to one, and to the person who'd committed the crime, whoever they were, was unnerving.

"Your father won't admit it, but he's shaken. He was tossing and turning all night and shouting in his sleep. It reminds me of when he used to return from military tours to Northern Ireland."

Dotty remembered her father being absent, and missing birthdays and Christmases, but not where he'd been.

"And of course it's all over the papers, with the victim being an MSP, and a controversial one at that." Karen sat down on Dotty's bed and stroked the still sleeping Earl Grey.

"Why was she so controversial?" queried Dotty.

"She was a strong advocate for an independent Scotland."

"But I thought most Scottish people want to be free of England."

Earl Grey started purring. A deep, contented sound.

"They're pretty much split fifty-fifty and have been for years. Your father and I, like many people, just want to get on with things. We have a Scottish Parliament and representation in Westminster, so it's the best of both worlds. I wish MSPs would concentrate on the real issues we Scots face. There's a drug crisis, and education and health services are struggling too. I'm sure it's easier to tackle them as part of the UK, rather than Scotland alone."

"But are there fanatics so against independence that they'd kill over it? I thought everyone had to vote in a referendum before there can be a change."

Karen moved her hand from Earl Grey and smoothed down the top of the duvet cover.

"There are some issues where feelings are running high. Take the military, for example. When your dad joined, he swore allegiance to the Queen. He's adamant he'd never do the same to a President of Scotland, or whatever position the leader would hold. Historically, it wouldn't be right."

Karen was interrupted by the sound of the doorbell. She checked her watched and wrinkled her brow. "I wonder who's calling at quarter past nine on a Saturday morning. Probably a delivery."

She stood up, but as she reached the door, she asked, "Shall I make scrambled eggs for breakfast?"

Dotty gave her mother a tentative smile. She never offered to cook. "That would be nice."

Karen closed the bedroom door, but as Dotty pulled herself out of bed, she heard voices on the other side and then a knock.

Karen poked her head around the door and said, "There's a policewoman to see you. I said you were still in bed, but she said not to worry, she can interview you in your pyjamas."

"Dotty," called a female voice. "It's me, Morag."

Dotty nodded at Karen and placed her feet in a pair of tartan slippers. She found a white waffle dressing gown hanging on the back of the door and wrapped it around herself, tying the cord at her waist.

Morag was wearing her police uniform of black trousers and a shirt with a high-vis vest.

Dotty placed her mug of tea on the circular kitchen table as Karen placed another beside it and said, "There you go, Morag. I'll wake Euan."

"Shall we?" asked Morag, pulling out a kitchen chair and sitting down. "Och, what a night. I've barely slept a wink. Good job Davy was staying at my mum's. But I doubt I'll be finished in time to take him to curling practice this afternoon."

"Curling?" queried Dotty.

"A great Scottish sport, and probably the only one we win any medals in. It's like bowls on ice, but not ten-pin bowling, the other type. You should try it while you're here. Anyway, getting back to the case."

She lowered her voice as she confided, "I'm in the doghouse for letting it happen on my watch. That's why it's my job to interview witnesses rather than have my day off. But when Assistant Chief Constable Rhona Cameron asks you to jump, you dinnae ask how high."

Dotty smiled, despite the seriousness of the situation. She liked Morag, who she classed as the conscientious walking-the-beat type of police officer. There were certainly no frills, and what you saw was what you got.

"So who do you think killed Iona McDuff?" asked Morag.

"I've still no idea. It was just too dark to see. But what about the stage victim, the woman with the white hat sitting near me? Who killed her?"

"The man with the tweed cap and holes in his jumper. The actor is Toby Mills. I'm sure you've heard of him?"

Dotty shook her head.

"Toby Mills," repeated Karen as she closed her bedroom door and strode towards them. "He was in that TV series, *Driftwood Cove*?"

Morag turned towards Karen, who was removing items from the

fridge. "That's right. One of the original characters from when it started nearly twenty-five years ago."

Karen held a box of eggs as she turned to Morag, her eyes sparkling as she asked, "Do you think his daughter, Coral, really blew up his yacht?"

"No, I'm sure it was his business partner," replied Morag.

Dotty picked up her mug of tea, bewildered by the conversation.

Karen carried the eggs to the counter and Morag turned back to Dotty. "You've no idea what we're talking about, have you?"

"Sorry, no."

"Toby Mills is a well-known actor who was supposed to be playing the murderer last night. His TV character was recently killed off, which he told me is the only reason he'd agreed to be in the play."

"I might have to watch this play, if it's allowed to continue," said Karen as she noisily removed a metal baking tray from a pile of baking tins in a cupboard. "Bacon and scrambled eggs?" she asked Morag.

"Och, I would'nae say no. All I had time to grab this morning was a cup of coffee and a slice of toast. And after only four hours sleep."

"Will the play be allowed to continue?" asked Dotty.

"That decision's above my pay grade, but I heard the ACC telling the Scene Examination Team in no uncertain terms that they were to work the weekend. And that play's not the only performance happening in the Side Theatre this year. There's bound to be pressure to open it up again. The show must go on and all that."

Morag placed a sketched plan on the table. "This is where I think everyone was when the lights came on. That cross is our victim, Iona McDuff, and next to her is Lord Willoughby Thorpe. And your dad was standing at the back here, next to an empty hand hold."

"That's not right," realised Dotty, turning the plan to face her. "Dad and I were the last to enter the makeshift carriage. I remember Dad hesitating as the only space we could see, which didn't involve pushing past people to sit in the empty seats, was beside the MSP. She was standing at the back of the carriage, not sitting down, and Dad took the place next to her."

Morag turned the plan back to face her and asked, "So you and the other guests weren't told specifically where to go?"

"No, we weren't, although Iona McDuff might have been, and she made sure she was the first person from the front row to enter the makeshift carriage. Skye, the assistant producer, told us to find a place marked by a luminous yellow sticker. By the time I entered to find a place, the young man with the black leather jacket had started speaking. Luckily, I spotted a sticker on the rail, just inside the doorway, so I grabbed that."

"This is you?" Morag tapped a spot marked with a DS on the plan. Dotty craned her neck to make sure it was beside the correct door. "Yes, that was me. I was near the play's victim."

Dotty had left her bedroom door ajar and Earl Grey now pushed himself through the gap and sauntered into the kitchen, stopping beside Karen and rubbing against her legs.

"What a beautiful cat," exclaimed Morag, "But he's huge."

Dotty stood and went to pick up Earl Grey. As she sat down again, holding her furry companion, she replied, "You're not as fat as you used to be, are you? Not after chasing rodents around those French fields. But begging for bacon and not exercising while you're here means you'll pile on the pounds again."

Earl Grey's large yellow eyes gave her an accusatory stare.

Karen shook her head. "Is that why he appeared? Because he smelt bacon?"

"Sensible animal," muttered Euan, emerging from his bedroom. "You wanted to see me, Constable?"

CHAPTER ELEVEN

"Euan!" exclaimed Karen as the egg she'd been holding smashed on the floor, its contents splattering across the oak floorboards.

In the small kitchen of their flat, Euan had bumped into her whilst trying to prepare a cafetière of coffee.

"Shoo." She waved her hand, indicating for him to move. "Why don't you all sit at the dining table so I can finish preparing breakfast in peace?"

Dotty placed Earl Grey on the floor and helped her dad pull the dining table away from the wall as Morag pushed Euan's leather chair out of the way.

Karen added, "Just give me ten minutes. Dotty dear, when you have a chance, can you lay the table?"

Her mother's domesticity surprised and impressed Dotty, as did her pragmatic approach to the morning's events.

Dotty was used to police officers popping in and out, as her friends in the police force had done when she lived in the Cotswolds, but for most people, entertaining a police officer who was making enquiries into a recent murder would be alarming.

Sitting at the dining table, Morag turned to Euan and said, "Mr Abercrombie, I was discussing with your daughter the position of those on stage last night when Ms McDuff was killed. And I understand she was initially standing next to you. Why did she move?"

"Call me Euan, and I've no idea why she moved. But I did hear her call out."

Dotty remembered the voice in the darkness. So it had been the victim's voice.

"Call out what?" pressed Morag.

"I think she cried, 'I don't like this', or something like that," Dotty answered.

Euan looked at his daughter, his eyes widening and, with a note of awe in his voice, said, "That's exactly what she said. Well remembered."

"And do you know why, Euan? Did she say anything when you took your place, or did she whisper anything during the performance?"

Euan shook his head. "She was fine, preening like a peacock until the lights went out. It was a surprise, the sudden darkness after the bright stage lights. I was a bit shocked myself, but then, it was only a play."

His words hung in the air.

Morag sucked the end of her pen, her head to one side as she stared up at the ceiling. Removing the pen, she mused, "So our victim initially stood at the back of the makeshift carriage, but when the lights came back on she was seated. When did she move?"

Dotty wasn't sure if Morag was muttering to herself or whether she expected an answer.

"I felt rather than heard people shifting positions in the dark," Euan said, "and I thought I heard … but that can't be right."

Morag fixed Euan with an intense stare, but her tone was encouraging and soft as she asked, "Thought you heard what?"

"Here you go. Fresh coffee." Karen placed a cafetière on the table along with a white milk jug. "Dotty?" She raised her eyebrows.

"In a minute," replied Dotty, without looking up. She was concentrating on her father.

As Karen returned to the kitchen, Euan said, "Footsteps on the stage. But they sounded far away, not next to me."

"Dotty," called Karen with an insistent note that Dotty felt she couldn't ignore.

Dotty returned to the dining table with cups, the sugar bowl, and teaspoons. She heard Morag say, "But Ms McDuff must have moved to the seat while the lights were off."

Dotty studied the plan which Morag had placed on the table again and said, "Willoughby Thorpe should know when Ms McDuff moved, as he was sitting in the place where she was found. He must have shuffled across to the spare place to let her sit down."

"Dotty," called Karen again, a note of irritation in her voice.

Dotty busied herself laying the table and making toast. Earl Grey snaked around her and her mother's legs until Karen exclaimed, "Get this cat out of here."

"Sorry, boy, but I'll save you some bacon." Dotty carried Earl Grey into her bedroom.

"Meow," Earl Grey complained as she closed the door.

"That is one greedy cat," remarked Karen.

"He's used to being fed titbits when people are cooking," Dotty defended Earl Grey as she picked up the toast rack and carried it to the dining table.

Morag and Euan were discussing where other witnesses were when the lights went out.

Finally, Dotty helped her mother carry plates of scrambled egg and streaky bacon over to the dining table. Karen also removed a plastic container of cherry tomatoes and a bag of mixed lettuce leaves from the fridge and placed them next to her plate.

"This is wonderful, thank you," said Morag when everyone was sitting down.

"Toast?" Euan offered.

Morag took two pieces as Karen opened the bag of lettuce leaves and added a handful of its contents to her plate. She declined the toast. "So tell me more about the *Driftwood Cove* actor, Toby Mills."

Morag spluttered through a mouthful of toast and scrambled egg, "Thinks a bit too much of himself."

She finished chewing and added, "And he was furious about what happened last night, and that the play can't continue until the powers that be give their approval. Personally, I think he was irked to be upstaged. He was playing the murderer."

CHAPTER TWELVE

On Sunday morning, Dotty woke at seven and, becoming aware of the sunshine behind her grey curtains, decided she shouldn't waste the day.

She hadn't done much on Saturday after Morag's visit, although she had enjoyed spending time with both her parents and had cooked them chicken Provençale, a classic French recipe she'd learned, for supper.

But today she was determined to experience something of Edinburgh.

Pottering through to the kitchen in her pyjamas, she was surprised to find Karen sitting at the kitchen table, her laptop open in front of her.

"Morning," Karen said brightly. "I'm getting some work done and then I thought it would be nice to visit the National Portrait Gallery. It's my favourite, and they have a lovely coffee shop on the ground floor."

Once again, Dotty was surprised, not by her mother's organisation, but by her suggestion to visit something cultural and that they should do so together. And even more so, that this seemed normal to her mother.

Dotty thought Karen only visited bars and restaurants with her friends, or fitness and yoga classes.

"I'd like that," agreed Dotty, "Although as the weather's so nice, I'd prefer not to be inside all day."

Karen glanced down the room at the patio doors. "It is lovely, isn't it? I wonder if Euan would drive us down to Melrose to explore the Abbey and have a late lunch at the Queen of Scots?"

At ten o'clock, the front doors of the National Portrait Gallery opened, and Dotty and Karen stepped inside the red brick, Gothic style building.

"I'll pay for this," offered Dotty.

"No need," smiled Karen. "It's free. But you can buy coffee later." She opened a wooden door and Dotty followed her.

"Wow. This isn't what I was expecting." Dotty gazed up at the double-height room with an internal quadrangle of stone columns and arches supporting a gallery above.

A frieze decorated the wall above the arches which appeared to be figures, mostly men but with some women and children, marching one behind the other. It was ornate, with a gold background, which matched the gilt wreaths encircling the tops of the columns.

"The figures represent Scottish history," whispered Karen, "And they march in chronological order."

A large marble statue of a man was facing Dotty and her footsteps echoed on the mosaic floor as she crossed to read the inscription. It was the famous Scottish poet, Robert Burns.

She enjoyed the gallery, which consisted of several themed rooms. One was devoted to Mary Queen of Scots, and the Stuart Royal family descended from her. Another, probably Dotty's favourite, was full of portraits of recent people in Scottish history, including the actor, Sean Connery, and two suffragettes her mother was keen to show her.

She was less impressed by the death masks in a room laid out as a library.

Dotty was ready for a refreshing cup of tea when they'd finished their tour and Karen led them back to the ground floor and a large room near the entrance.

As Dotty carried her tray with tea for herself and a black coffee for Karen, and two Scottish shortbread biscuits, she saw a man enter whom she recognised.

Of course, it was Lord Thorpe who'd worn the pinstripe suit in the play. He was accompanied by the woman she'd seen briefly in police uniform, and the actor, Toby Mills, whom they'd discussed the previous day.

"I'll buy," declared Lord Thorpe, in his upper-class English accent.

As Dotty sat down Karen whispered, "That's Lord Willoughby Thorpe."

"I know, he was in the play," Dotty whispered back, "and so were the other two."

"The man's Toby Mills, and the woman's a stand-up comedian called Jenny Church. Some friends and I have tickets to see her one-woman show in a couple of weeks. It's all about menopausal and older women, and it's supposed to be hysterical, although she does use strong language."

More people entered the busy cafe and sat down, forcing Toby Mills and Jenny Church to take a free table next to Dotty and Karen.

Dotty picked up a piece of shortbread and bit into it. So wonderfully crisp and buttery at the same time.

"So what do you think?" asked Karen.

Still savouring her shortbread Dotty was puzzled by the question. "About what?"

"The gallery."

"Oh, it's amazing. And Flora Drummond, the suffragette, sounded a fascinating person."

"Not someone to be ignored. She was very strong-willed, and knew what she wanted," replied Karen. "And someone else who has impressed me these past few days is you."

"Me?" spluttered Dotty through a mouthful of shortbread. "What have I done?"

"I guess it's more what you haven't. There have been no hysterics or theatrics about witnessing a murder. In fact, quite the opposite. You've been clear-headed, remembering the event clearly and making well-thought-out observations and deductions. Just like a real detective."

Dotty felt her cheeks flush.

"This is ridiculous," Toby Mills muttered from the next table. "How long do the police need to scour the set for clues? I wish I'd never agreed to do this play."

"You agreed," admonished Jenny, swinging her head of dark shoulder-length hair round as she searched for someone or something at the serving counter, "because Willow launched your career. And with this play."

Jenny returned her attention to Toby, who was lounging on his chair with his feet resting on the one at the end of the table. She continued, "And maybe he can perform another miracle and relaunch it. I don't know why you're moaning. It's not as if you have any other options."

"Unlike you, I suppose you mean," Toby snapped back.

"I'm delighted to be part of Willow's farewell production. He and Suzie have been so supportive over the years, when I never thought my show would go further than regional theatres and working mens' clubs. I wish Suzie was well enough to travel, but perhaps it's better she's not here, after what's happened."

"You two managing to get along?" enquired Lord Willoughby Thorpe as he plonked a black tray down on the table.

Dotty didn't know whether she should think of him as Lord Thorpe or Willoughby Thorpe. He wasn't exactly dressed as a lord, wearing shorts and a T-shirt with New Model Army emblazoned across it.

A phone rang.

"Yes, speaking," said Willoughby Thorpe, answering his call.

He sat up. "That's excellent news." A pause. "Tomorrow. Thank you."

"What's up, Willow?" asked Jenny, swirling the tab of her tea bag around her cup.

Willoughby Thorpe gave her and Toby a huge smile. "That was the police. We're back in business."

CHAPTER THIRTEEN

On Monday morning, Dotty, who was still wearing her pyjamas, joined Karen at the kitchen table.

She sat down with her mug of tea as Karen, dressed in white shirt and navy pinstripe trousers, put down her phone and picked up her cup of black coffee.

"Did you enjoy yesterday?" asked Karen.

"The portrait gallery was fabulous, and it was nice to get out of Edinburgh and see some of the countryside, especially as it was so warm and sunny."

"I'm afraid it's grey and overcast today. What will you do?"

Dotty peered down the living space to the French windows. At least there was no rain splattering against them.

"I'd like to walk up to the Royal Mile, to see what's going on, and come back via the National Gallery of Scotland."

"Is that the one with the famous picture of the skating vicar?" asked Karen.

"Yes, and Edward Landseer's fabulous painting of a red stag, entitled 'Monarch of the Glen'."

Karen's phone bleeped. She gulped another mouthful of coffee and stood up. "Help yourself to breakfast and lunch. I'm working all week, but look through the festival brochure and see if there's anything you'd like to see one evening." She picked up her canvas briefcase and left the flat.

"Meow," cried Earl Grey, padding into the kitchen.

"OK. I'll sort out your breakfast and then I'll have a shower and get dressed."

An hour later, at just after eight o'clock, Dotty was once again sipping tea at the kitchen table. She'd showered, dressed, and eaten a bowl of muesli with yoghurt and fresh fruit.

Barefooted and unshaven, Euan joined her. "What's the plan for today?" he asked.

"I'm going to explore some of the Old Town and visit an art gallery. I know that's not really your thing, so I'm happy to go on my own."

"Are you sure?" queried Euan, scratching his chin. "But what about all the people, and you might get lost?"

"Dad, don't fret. I'm quite capable of visiting places by myself and I can either use my phone or ask someone if I'm unsure where I am. But what are you going to do?"

Euan crossed his arms. "I was going to spend the day with my daughter, but if she doesn't want to be with me …"

"Dad. Stop it. We had a great time yesterday, all of us together, but today I want to visit places I know you won't enjoy. I'd just feel guilty about dragging you round and then I'll rush and miss things. But is there anywhere you'd like us to go together later this week?"

"Whisky tasting," muttered Euan.

Dotty replied brightly, trying to appease her dad. "I'm not sure I like whisky, but that sounds fascinating. Just the two of us, or Mum as well?"

"I'll speak to her," Euan replied, as he stood up and carried his cup of coffee back to his bedroom.

Dotty felt her chest constrict. She had enjoyed spending the weekend with both her parents, despite the dreadful event on Friday evening, but there were places she'd looked up and wanted to visit which she knew her father would moan about. Today was her day, she thought brightly, pushing down the twinge of guilt she felt.

As she stood up to wash her mug, the doorbell rang.

Glancing at her parents' bedroom door, which remained closed, she entered the hallway and opened the front door.

"Sorry, it's me again," apologised a uniformed Morag with a lopsided smile.

"Come in," invited Dotty. "I can make you toast and tea or coffee, but there's no cooked breakfast today."

Morag chortled. "I don't visit you just for the food, although I really needed those eggs and bacon yesterday. Davy and I shared Scotch pancakes this morning, so I'm stuffed."

Dotty grinned, and as they entered the kitchen, said, "I thought real Scots only ate porridge for breakfast."

"Och, in the winter," replied Morag in a serious tone, but her eyes sparkled.

"Tea or coffee?" asked Dotty.

Morag tilted her head and after a pause replied, "Tea, I think. Milk, one sugar."

As Dotty prepared fresh cups of tea for them both, Morag explained, "I've come to tell you that the procurator fiscal has given permission for the play to continue." She looked expectantly at Dotty.

Dotty smiled back weakly.

"Did you already know that?" asked Morag, slightly deflated.

As Dotty finished making tea, she told Morag of the conversation she'd overheard in the National Portrait Gallery the previous day.

"Oh," said Morag, and then more keenly, "What did you think of Toby Mills and Jenny Church?"

They sat down and Dotty said, "You were right about Toby Mills, he is self-centred, but Jenny is an interesting character."

"And a hilarious stand-up comic. We should watch her show."

"I'd like that," agreed Dotty.

"But back to the play," said Morag in a businesslike tone.

"The ACC has tasked me to oversee its remaining performances and, after the events of Friday night, the condition of it opening is that nobody from the audience is allowed up on stage. The theatre group are looking for volunteers for the non-speaking parts and I thought of you."

"Me?" cried Dotty in surprise. "But why?"

"I can't, as I have to patrol the main theatre and backstage."

Morag locked eyes with Dotty and, in a frank tone, said, "But I need someone I can trust out there. And you're not police, so the cast, and more importantly the killer, won't be panicked by your presence. And you demonstrated on Saturday that you are observant and shrewd. Also, I can't be at the theatre all day as I have interviews to follow up."

"But …" Dotty began.

Morag continued, "And it's only for five performances. The play finishes on Friday evening. And think of the experience of being part of an Edinburgh Fringe production. Not everyone has that opportunity."

"I was going sightseeing today, and visiting the National Gallery," Dotty said lamely.

"I'm sure you still can. You won't be needed all day, and you can soon wander up to the Royal Mile from the Pleasance and see the street performers, or enjoy the atmosphere of the Pleasance Courtyard."

"But what if I'm given the part of the victim?"

"You won't be." Morag looked sympathetically at Dotty. "The lady who played that role on Friday has asked to keep it. Which is good news, as she's also a suspect, so we can keep an eye on her. Actually, I think she was disappointed that her moment was overshadowed by Iona McDuff's death, and she wants to know why Toby Mill's character shot her."

Dotty was silent. It was a fantastic opportunity, and being on stage on Friday hadn't been as terrifying as she'd expected. In fact, she hadn't had time to notice the audience. But she might this time, if the play ran its course.

Something inside her stirred. The part that hadn't stirred since she'd left the Cotswolds. The part that excitedly told her the game was afoot. That this was her opportunity to be involved in a high-level murder investigation of a prominent Scottish figure. She tried not to smile to herself.

"So you'll do it," announced Morag and, without waiting for an answer added, "and I have a task for you."

Dotty hesitated. She hoped it wasn't spying on someone, or worse still, following them.

"I need you to look for the gun the killer used. The Scene Examination Team didn't find it, and it might be crucial to the investigation."

"What about the stage gun?"

"We checked the one used on Friday, and the spare. Both have solid plastic barrels, so they couldn't even squirt water. They might look the part from a distance, but they're not even close to being real guns."

Morag looked pleadingly at Dotty, who breathed in deeply and sighed. "OK. I'll do it."

CHAPTER FOURTEEN

Morag gave Dotty a lift to the Pleasance in her compact electric police car. Glancing in the back, Dotty wasn't sure what Morag would do if she arrested anyone over five foot ten, as they wouldn't fit in her vehicle.

The journey was slow, with queues at the many traffic lights, but she enjoyed Morag's commentary of Edinburgh's sights and landmarks.

They didn't use the main theatre entrance but instead went in through the stage door, which led to an emergency exit next to the front of the stage. The theatre looked dingy in the daylight and Dotty noticed several stains on the carpet next to the first row of seats.

"It's not like that. My character needs to be at the front of the stage," Toby Mills demanded.

A younger man Dotty didn't recognise, with a shaved head, replied in an exasperated tone, "This scene is not about your character, Toby. Stay at the back."

Tensions were clearly running high.

"Officer," called the upper-class accent of Willoughby Thorpe, as he strode across the stage towards Dotty and Morag.

He dropped down, perching on the edge of the wooden stage.

"Thank you for persuading the necessary people to allow us to continue with our play."

"That wasn't my doing, sir. More likely the ACC," Morag replied.

Willoughby Thorpe nodded his head. "I suspect you're right. And who have we here?" he asked, smiling warmly at Dotty.

"My friend Dotty, who was part of your performance on Friday, and has agreed to be part of your company this week."

"Marvellous," exclaimed Willoughby, jumping down and thrusting out his hand for Dotty to shake. "And you must call me Willow. Everyone else does and I find things get done quicker when everyone isn't trying to use my full name and title. And what about you, Officer? Will you be part of our merry crew?"

"I'll certainly be around during performances, but not on stage."

"That's a shame, but come and meet everyone." Willow led them up a set of steps onto the stage. "I'm sure you know Toby, by reputation, and Jenny."

Toby scowled, but Jenny tilted her head and asked, "Have we met before?"

"I was one of the VIP guests on stage on Friday," replied Dotty. She didn't admit that she'd been listening in to their conversation at the Portrait Gallery too.

"And this is young Robbie, our actor producer." Willow introduced Dotty and Morag to the shaven-headed young man.

"And what part do you play?" asked Morag.

"I'm the young rocker with the black leather jacket and the hair."

Morag stared at Robbie's shaved head and frowned.

"It's a wig," he explained.

Dotty realised he'd been the one speaking when she'd found her place in the makeshift train carriage on Friday night, and he must have been sitting opposite Iona McDuff's dead body.

Morag was staring up at the lighting rig, and Dotty wondered if her mind was on the same track as Dotty's.

"I need to speak to you, Mr ?" said Morag.

"Campbell. Robert Campbell," replied Robbie, "But it'll have to wait until we've finished this run through, otherwise we'll never be ready for this evening. Why don't you take a seat?"

Robbie turned to Dotty and said, "And as Skye's away searching for friends and fellow students to fill in the gaps in our crew, can you take over at the controls?"

"Excellent idea," barked Willow, returning to his place on the stage.

Dotty followed Robbie across the stage and into the curtained wings at the left-hand side. They passed behind the curtains and climbed three steps into the raised control booth. "It's relatively simple, as there are only three things you need to do," Robbie instructed.

"This switch turns the lights on and off. This dial makes the train noises, and this one the brakes, and press this button for the sound of the doors opening and shutting. Don't worry about the station announcements. I'll do that."

Dotty didn't think it sounded at all simple, and that was four things, not three, but Robbie left her and called, "Train noise."

She turned the dial.

"Lights off," instructed Robbie, and the rehearsal continued.

Robbie called, "And turn all the lights on."

Flushing and feeling the sweat under her arms, Dotty flicked all the switches. One turned on a fan, which she quickly switched off.

"So that's how the play ends," said Morag, as she approached Dotty's booth.

Someone turned on the main theatre lights.

"You can turn everything off," directed Robbie.

Relieved, Dotty flicked switches. At the end of one row, she noticed the corner of a photograph sticking out of the control panel. Her curiosity getting the better of her, she tugged at it and pulled out a colour image of Skye and a pale-looking woman. Her mother?

Dotty replaced the photograph.

"Let's reconvene at four," instructed Robbie. "And no liquid lunches."

"Mr Campbell, shall we have our interview?" asked Morag in a tone that left no opportunity to refuse.

Robbie nodded in a resigned manner and approached the edge of the stage, sitting down on the edge of it. "What would you like to know?"

"You were sitting opposite Iona McDuff when she was found dead."

"That's right. When the lights went out, a woman cried out and I heard and felt some scuffling, but I couldn't see anything. I was surprised to find myself sitting opposite the MSP instead of Willow. He'd shuffled across to the empty seat."

"Yes, he told me he'd felt a hand push at him and a woman whisper to him to move over. He wasn't sure what was happening, but he did as requested," acknowledged Morag.

Dotty had remained motionless in the control booth. So she was right. She had felt people moving about in the darkness. She ducked down, hoping not to be noticed so she could continue to listen to the interview.

As she did, she noted a piece of paper tucked into a gap underneath the control panels. Had it been purposefully hidden?

"Did you know Iona McDuff was dead when the lights came back on?" asked Morag.

"No. I blinked a few times before I realised she was staring at me in a most disconcerting way. It's only when someone shouted that she was dead that I understood."

"Do you know who shouted?"

"Sorry, no."

Dotty carefully removed the folded sheet of paper from its hiding place under the controls and opened it up. Perhaps it had just got stuck rather than hidden as it only showed the position of actors during the murder scene in the play.

There were initials for Toby Mills, a large 'W' for Willow and crosses where she presumed the guest actors might be standing or sitting. Towards the bottom left corner was the number '20' and above it '15', which didn't mean anything to Dotty.

"Was Iona McDuff briefed beforehand about where to stand?" asked Morag.

"No, we left the guests to choose their own places," replied Robbie.

Then Iona had been very clear she wanted to be in the centre of the stage, thought Dotty.

"How many shots did you hear?" said Morag.

"Just the one, but it was very loud. It made my ears ring."

Probably the shot from the real gun, thought Dotty as she stuffed the folded paper back into its hiding place.

"Finally, do you have, or know anyone who has, a reason to harm Ms McDuff?"

Dotty stood up and saw Robbie shake his head and reply, "Absolutely not."

CHAPTER FIFTEEN

"Be back by three," were Robbie's parting words as Dotty and Morag left the Pleasance Side theatre.

"I can't see that Mr Campbell had a reason to shoot Iona McDuff. Quite the opposite since it's had such an impact on his play, but I'll find out more when I return to the station," remarked Morag.

"How will you find out more?" asked Dotty, her brow wrinkling.

"I'm the one who has to do the running around. I'm not sure if it's to keep me away from the ACC or because I was at the theatre when the incident occurred and know those involved." Morag tilted her head and looked up at the grey clouds.

"So?" pressed Dotty.

"Sorry," apologised Morag, focusing on Dotty again as they reached her small police car.

"So the rest of the team is digging into the background of everyone who was performing or watching the play, going through my interviews, and following up leads. That's why I should know more about the case when we come back for this evening's performance. And I hope nothing violent happens. I'm bringing Davy with me as mum's playing bingo."

Dotty felt a drop of rain on her hand.

"Do you want a lift?" asked Morag.

Dotty had been about to walk up to the Royal Mile but, if it was going to rain, she'd be better off inside, looking at paintings. "Can you drop me at the National Gallery?"

"Sure, jump in."

The Scottish National Gallery was another imposing neo-classical stone building, located between Edinburgh's old and new towns. Dotty wondered if the railway tracks ran beneath it.

"The entrance is round the side, opposite the Royal Academy," called Morag, before Dotty thanked her for the lift and closed the car door.

The sky darkened and Dotty hurried after other visitors, also seeking sanctuary from the weather in the art gallery. She climbed the stone steps between two vintage lamp posts, towards the large blue banners hanging between the building's stone columns, which left her in no doubt she was in the right place.

She entered and was once again told that admission was free, but donations were welcome. She pushed a five-pound note into a large glass box before entering what she realised was a series of rooms separated by arches.

The first was painted a vivid red, and it was hung with a mixture of paintings, from women in their eighteenth-century splendour to dramatic biblical scenes. At the centre of the room, a marble statue vividly represented two young women wearing floaty dresses.

After an hour happily wandering around the rooms, Dotty's stomach gurgled so she asked an attendant, "Is there a cafe here?"

"There are two," the middle-aged man smiled back. "Downstairs, at garden level, we have a wonderful restaurant serving classic Scottish dishes, but you might need to book a table in advance, and back at the entrance we have the Cafe Espresso serving delicious cakes and food on the go."

"Thank you," said Dotty, making her way back to the entrance and Cafe Espresso.

Having enjoyed a cup of tea and a scone piled with jam and cream, she returned to the gallery. As she admired 'The Monarch of the Glen' painting for the third time, she heard someone say, "It's half-past two. Didn't we say we'd meet gran at three?"

Dotty realised she needed to make a move if she was to arrive at the Pleasance in time for the afternoon rehearsal.

Outside it was still grey, but at least it wasn't raining, so she walked up the road Morag had driven down earlier, passing the Museum on the Mound before entering the old town. It was quite a climb, and she had to stop at the top to take a breath.

Crowds of people packed the pavements of the Royal Mile but at least the section to her left, which Morag had suggested she use if she walked back to the Pleasance, was cordoned off with metal crash barriers and a sign informing drivers it was closed to traffic.

Dotty joined the meandering crowd and passed under the large 'Fringe' sign which spanned the road. Groups of people surrounded performers pretending to be statues or riding tall unicycles. More young people were thrusting leaflets into the hands of passers-by.

Dotty had to rush to reach the theatre in time and, as she entered, she peeled off her raincoat, hoping to cool down and lose the flush in her cheeks from dashing up the hill to the Pleasance.

Young people were standing on their own or in pairs in front of the stage.

A few minutes later, Willow walked onto the stage and beamed down at them all. "Welcome, welcome. It's fantastic to see you and I hope you enjoy your few days with us. I think Skye has explained that the play is called *Underground Murder* and the first act is set on a London tube train."

There was muttering from the students, and the emergency door near Dotty opened.

"Each of you will have several roles, but don't worry, you won't have to speak. Robbie, our esteemed producer, will be with you shortly."

As Willow exited the stage, Dotty realised the latecomer was the lady who'd played the stage victim at the previous performance. Dotty looked across at her and smiled. The woman was younger than Dotty remembered, but she had been wearing a vintage white hat.

The woman approached Dotty and whispered, "You were here on Friday, weren't you?"

"Yes, my dad and I were both invited, well actually we weren't personally asked, but we had VIP tickets," garbled Dotty.

"I wasn't invited either, but as my father, the judge, was out of town, I took his place and came with his assistant." She looked around before lowering her voice, "And I was enjoying myself until someone shouted that Iona McDuff was dead. I'm Sheena, by the way."

"I'm Dotty. Is that why you agreed to come back? So you could you have a proper stab at the role?" Dotty winced at her choice of words.

"Agreed?" Sheena's voice rose in indignation. "I demanded to be given the role."

Robbie walked onto the stage and surveyed his new recruits as Skye entered her control booth.

"Who's been fiddling with my controls?" demanded Skye.

Robbie replied in an off-hand manner, "As you weren't here, I asked one of the stand-ins to do the lights and sounds."

"Who?" demanded Skye.

The theatre had fallen silent, and Dotty felt her cheeks flush again as she turned and looked up at Skye. "Me," she replied nervously, and then she gushed, "And I'm sorry if I messed things up and didn't put them back as you like them, but I wasn't really sure what I was doing."

Skye regarded Dotty and then her face softened. "I suppose that's all right then." She ducked under the control panel.

Robbie gave a shaky laugh. "Now that's cleared up, let's get on with the rehearsal. Sheena?"

"I'm here," waved Sheena, beside Dotty.

"Come and take your place, and it's Dotty, isn't it?" said Robbie.

Dotty nodded her head.

"You come and sit opposite Sheena."

Sheena and Dotty took their places on the right-hand set of seats as Robbie arranged the new recruits around them.

"You will all enter at the same time, at London Victoria, and find your places. The actors will already have taken their seats."

Robbie made them run through the entrance to the carriage scene and the murder, where Sheena excelled at being a dead body, several times before announcing, "I think you've got that. Take a break while I check if Jenny's back. She said she'd come in early to run through some of her scenes with you."

Sheena leaned forward and said to Dotty, "This might actually be fun if the performance isn't interrupted again. And Josh, my father's assistant, is trying to persuade the judge to come and watch on Friday night when he's back from his trip."

"Jenny's here," announced Robbie, walking back onto the stage. "First, we'll need someone to play her sergeant."

Several pairs of eager hands shot into the air.

"Dotty, why don't you do that? All you have to do is follow her around, pretend to make notes and don't get in her or the other actors' way."

Dotty gulped. She'd learned this morning that when Robbie said something was easy, it wasn't.

For the next half an hour, Dotty followed Jenny about the stage as she questioned suspects and Dotty pretended to make notes.

"Dotty," called Robbie. "Here." He held up a pair of handcuffs. Being careful not to get in the way of any actors, and still paying attention to the action on the stage, Dotty made a grab for the handcuffs.

Not concentrating, she mistakenly hit a canvas sandbag which was attached to a rope ascending into the roof space. The sandbag swung towards Robbie, who dodged it and gave Dotty the handcuffs.

Jenny was waiting for Dotty to pass her the handcuffs, and when she'd received them, she arrested the overly dramatic Toby Mills. As Dotty led Toby off stage, a beaming Morag appeared in the wings.

"You're a natural," she praised Dotty.

"Hardly," sniped Toby.

Morag surveyed him, her eyes narrowing. "Actually, it's rather apt you're in handcuffs. According to my colleagues, you've been getting yourself into trouble in the run-up to the festival, so we need to have a little chat."

Morag took hold of the handcuffs, still attached to Toby's arms, and escorted him behind the stage curtains. Before Dotty could follow them, Robbie shouted, "Dotty? We're waiting for you."

After another twenty minutes, Robbie appeared satisfied and called an end to rehearsals. "Take a short break and then see Skye about costumes. We don't have complete sets for you, but we'll give you props so the audience knows who you represent."

Dotty was sipping from a plastic water bottle when Morag joined her and muttered, "I still don't think he did it."

"Who?" asked Dotty.

"Toby Mills. But it wouldn't surprise me if my bosses drag him to the station for a formal interview. Now, where is Jenny Church?"

"Here," said Jenny, approaching them, carrying a selection of police hats. She placed a tall, dome-shaped one on Dotty's head, which slipped down and almost covered Dotty's eyes.

"Not that one." Jenny removed the first hat and placed a flat-topped one on Dotty. "That'll do, and here's a notebook for you to scribble in when I'm interviewing the suspects."

She handed Dotty a black, bound notebook with a pen attached to it with a piece of string. She also gave Dotty the handcuffs Toby had been wearing. "And I've asked Skye to find you a black police jacket, but she has loads to do at the moment and might not have it for this evening's performance."

"Did you want to see me?" Jenny turned to Morag.

Dotty left the pair but didn't go far, sitting down on a nearby chair, pretending to alter something on her police hat.

"My colleagues at the station have been running background checks on everyone and they've discovered you and Iona McDuff have a history."

"I'd hardly call it that," laughed Jenny.

Morag was not laughing. "I would. She's banned your stand-up show from the festival for the past four years ..."

"But not this year," interjected Jenny.

"No, because someone high-up applied pressure. They wouldn't tell me who, but I'm surprised Iona agreed considering the gags you made about her, independence, and women's rights."

Jenny dropped her hands to her side. "Look, my shows are aimed at women in their fifties who are jaded from life and their unappreciated stereotypical roles. Iona McDuff has no idea how they feel, and she was an easy target. And as for her banning my shows, it just made them more popular in London, and regional theatres."

Dotty glanced up and saw Morag nodding in understanding.

"Look, I didn't want her dead," insisted Jenny. "Now I have to find someone else to aim my jokes at, and why would I kill her the first year I'm actually allowed to perform at the festival?"

"It makes sense to me," agreed Morag, "but my superiors might not be so understanding. Don't leave Edinburgh without our authority."

"Oh, I have no intention of leaving. I've a play and a show to perform. Are you coming to see my show?"

Morag glanced across at Dotty and said, "We're considering it."

"Fabulous. I'll make sure you both get VIP tickets."

Dotty blanched at the suggestion. She'd had quite enough of VIP tickets.

CHAPTER SIXTEEN

Jenny Church left Morag standing on the stage, and Dotty sitting on a chair near her.

Morag joined Dotty and asked, "What do you think?"

"Her explanation sounded reasonable, although it's probably worth your colleagues looking into her further. And while I know she's an actor, she'd have to be a very good one to appear that relaxed and unconcerned in the circumstances."

"I agree," said Morag, tilting her head and looking up at the theatre's ceiling.

"Evening, Officer. Are you going to man the entrance and make sure no deranged killers are let loose in here tonight?" asked Willow, walking out onto the stage and smiling broadly.

"Lord Thorpe, the death of an MSP during your play is no laughing matter," Morag admonished.

"You're right, of course. She ruined our farewell tour." Willow wandered to the front of the stage and surveyed the empty seats. By the entrance, students were preparing for the audience to arrive.

"Twenty-five years ago, we first performed here. It wasn't this theatre. As an unknown theatrical group, we were given the Attic, but that only made it more intimate and dramatic."

"Whose idea was it to invite Iona McDuff?" Morag asked.

Willow turned to face her. "Mine, well actually my wife, Suzie's. She and Iona's mum were friends at university. Suzie can't be with us, as she's too ill to travel, and she's devastated by Iona's death. I thought I'd have to go home, but she insists I stay to see the play through to the finish and help find Iona's killer."

Willow sighed. "Suzie was so excited Iona had agreed not only to watch the play but also to take part in it."

"But were your own views different from those of your wife?" asked Morag. "After all, you and Ms McDuff had opposing political stances on Scottish Independence."

"I think the Union should remain together as it has for the past three hundred years. Before that, we were forever fighting. That's not a situation we should return to. Leave the brawls to the rugby pitch."

Morag's phone rang. She thanked Willow and walked away from Dotty as she answered her call.

Skye appeared and asked Dotty, "Do you have your outfit for the train and all the sergeant's props?"

"I'd better check," replied Dotty, and she and Skye left the main stage.

The backstage area was dingy and, even though Dotty knew Jenny and Skye had swept the floors thoroughly after the Scene Examination Team had finished, it still smelt musty.

She'd found a peg to hang her handcuffs and police hat on, together with a plastic shopping bag containing the notebook and pen, and the wig and glasses for the first scene.

She showed them all to Skye, who made a note on her tablet as she said, "I still need to find you a police jacket."

Skye moved on to talk to a group of students.

Morag's voice called through the stage curtains, "Dotty."

Dotty found Morag on stage standing with a boy of nine or ten who was peering at the makeshift train carriage and twisting his hand in Morag's.

"This is Davy," said Morag, as she tugged the boy's hand.

He turned to Dotty and smiled up at her. "Hi, are you one of the actors?"

"Not exactly. I will be on stage, but I have a non-speaking part."

"Awesome. Do you think I can be on stage, too?"

Willow, dressed in a pinstripe suit and carrying his briefcase, newspaper, and bowler hat, must have overheard as he walked up to Davy and said, "I'd love to give you a part, but the laws on child actors are very strict."

He looked around, and his attention was caught by Skye's control booth. "But there are no rules saying you can't help with the technical side."

Davy's eyes widened. "For real?" was all he said as Willow led him away.

Morag watched her son with a resigned expression. "I really should find a way to reconcile with his father. He needs a man in his life for guidance and direction."

"But you're doing a great job with him," Dotty responded.

Davy was on the top step leading to the control booth looking up at Skye, who was talking to Willow, as he stood behind Davy.

Skye smiled and stepped back so Davy could enter the cramped control booth.

"I bet he does a better job than I did," remarked Dotty.

"I'm just relieved he has something to do, and I don't have to worry about him during the performance. But now we better let the audience in." Morag strode up the side aisle and when she reached the entrance, the two students standing there opened the theatre doors.

Immediately, the noise of excited, chattering people filled the theatre and Dotty took it as her cue to return backstage and prepare for the play.

The play. People were coming to watch, and she would be acting on stage. It was the first time she'd thought of it like that, and her tummy churned. Oh dear. She wasn't sure she could do this.

"Everything OK?" Jenny asked brightly. She was wearing her police officer uniform and, with her hair drawn back into a tight bun, she looked just as intimidating as ACC Rhona Cameron.

"I think so," stammered Dotty.

"Stage fright," grinned Jenny. "That's normal. You won't see me just before I go out as you'll already be on stage, but I find it helps to concentrate on two things. Firstly, my feet. Feel them connected to the floor, which will help ground you. That's important, as you don't want to fall over as you walk onto the stage. And then think about your breathing and how it connects your whole body."

Dotty wriggled her toes, feeling her feet, and then breathed deeply in and out.

"It looks like we'll have a full house," declared Willow, whispering loudly. "Excellent."

Dotty continued to concentrate on her feet and her breathing as the sound swelled in the theatre. She hadn't felt this nervous on Friday night, but it had been different sitting in the audience, and she hadn't known what to expect.

Robbie bustled along the row of actors, positioned like Dotty next to their pegs or standing in small groups. He was wearing his black leather jacket and the pompadour style wig. "Everyone ready?" he asked.

CHAPTER SEVENTEEN

Dotty and the student stand-in actors stood at the back of the stage in the Pleasance Side Theatre and bowed again.

Dotty was relieved not to see people's faces in the audience during the performance, but now she'd like to see their reaction. Hopefully, the loud clapping was proof they'd enjoyed the play.

Willow stepped forward and held up a hand. The clapping subsided.

"Ladies and gentlemen. Thank you for coming this evening and supporting one of our last performances as a theatre group. As you may know, we performed this play twenty-five years ago at our Fringe debut."

Some people clapped, but Willow silenced them by raising his hand again and continuing, "But tonight's performance is dedicated to Iona McDuff. We are all devastated by her death." Willow paused for probably half a minute. Dotty presumed out of respect for Iona.

"Thank you once again. There will be four more performances of the play, so please tell your friends or join us for another showing of *Underground Murder*." Willow finished on a dramatic note as his spotlight was switched off and he left the stage.

Adrenaline pumped through Dotty's veins, and she looked

excitedly around at the students, who were hugging or slapping each other on the back.

"Well done," praised Jenny as she joined Dotty. "But relax a bit more and enjoy yourself. You were a bit stiff tonight."

"Just as I would be if I had to follow the ACC around," Morag remarked as she joined them. "Great show, and I wasn't expecting that twist at the end."

"I suppose that went well," Toby Mills said to Jenny as he removed his flat cap.

"Any trouble in the audience?" Dotty asked Morag.

Morag shook her head. "Good as gold."

"Mum," cried Davy, rushing towards them. "That was awesome. And Skye let me turn the lights on and off, and make the noise of the doors opening, and even turn the spotlights off at the end." His eyes sparkled and he couldn't keep still.

Willow walked back onto the stage and, facing his cast, said, "Can I have your attention?" When everyone had stopped talking, he continued, "Another group is performing in the theatre tomorrow afternoon, so before we leave, we need to dismantle the carriage. After that, let's meet for drinks in the Pleasance Courtyard. The first round's on me."

"I should hope every round's on him," muttered Toby.

After emptying the stage and tidying away their props, the cast left the theatre by the stage door.

There were far fewer people sitting around in the Courtyard than when Dotty had arrived for her afternoon rehearsal. The drizzle must have sent them indoors or back home.

"All the stages are showing performances at the moment," said Morag. "I think I should get you home, Davy, before things get rowdy in here."

"Not just yet," declared Willow, who had secured tables under two blue-topped gazebos. At least they would provide some shelter from the weather. "Davy is part of the crew now and we are celebrating an excellent performance. It was a full house so, as they say, there's no such thing as bad publicity."

Dotty felt Morag tense beside her.

"Come on, Davy." Morag grabbed her son's hand.

"No, Mum," protested Davy, pulling back at her. "Can't we stay just for a short time? Pleeease?"

Morag sighed. "Och, all right. But only for half an hour, max. I have to be at the station for an early morning briefing on the case."

Dotty and Morag both accepted plastic glasses of champagne. Or was it sparkling wine? And Skye handed Davy a can of Iron Bru.

Morag rolled her eyes but restrained herself from saying anything.

"Thanks, Skye," said Davy. It was clear he was infatuated with the pretty young assistant producer.

"I know what it's like to be dragged to work with my mum because she's trying to put food on the table and has nobody to babysit," Skye revealed.

"Does your dad not live with you and your mum, either?"

"He didn't, and now I'm on my own."

"Where's your mum?"

"She died last year."

Davy took hold of Skye's hand and said, "Sorry."

Skye sniffed. "Don't be. It was for the best. She was in a lot of pain." Skye squatted down so she could look Davy in the eye. "But you look after your mum. You're the man of the house. And you do as she tells you, work hard, and make the most of your life."

As Skye straightened up, Morag said, "Thank you for looking after him. He obviously enjoyed himself."

"No trouble, and I'll be happy for his help the rest of the week," said Skye.

"Are you studying drama?" asked Dotty.

Skye laughed. "No, I'm training to be a vet. But I helped a friend out at last year's festival and learned the technical production side. Besides, it's far better paid than handing out leaflets. My course is five years long, so I need a lot of money to fund it and my living costs."

"Are you paying all of it yourself?" asked Dotty, a note of awe in her voice.

"No, I'm lucky. A trust paid my school fees and they've agreed to cover my course fees and, when my mum died, to contribute towards my living costs."

Skye looked down at Davy. "But I never took any of it for granted and worked hard at school." She ruffled the young boy's hair. "Just as you need to."

His large eyes were sombre as he nodded. "I will." Then he yawned.

"Now it is time to take you home young man," insisted Morag. "And I'll see you tomorrow, Dotty, but hopefully not before breakfast."

CHAPTER EIGHTEEN

Dotty stayed at the Pleasance Courtyard for another hour or so, soaking up the atmosphere as audiences filed out of the various venues and, despite the rain, enjoyed a drink or a takeaway meal from one of the food vendors.

Dotty hadn't eaten much all day and she, Jenny, and Skye each enjoyed a dish from the Thai street food vendor. Skye ordered a vegetarian option while Jenny and Dotty chose satay chicken served with noodles and stir-fried vegetables.

"Are you coming on to the Seven Sisters?" Toby asked as they finished eating.

Skye shook her head. "No, I don't want to spend all my hard-earned cash."

"I'm meeting a friend," Jenny replied.

Dotty knew it was time she headed home. She left the Pleasance fully intending to walk back to her parent's flat, but when she saw a black taxi crawling along the road, she hailed it and jumped in. "Broughton Place, please," she told the driver.

The taxi avoided the old town, taking a circuitous route to her parent's flat.

When she entered the flat, Karen greeted her. "Enjoyable evening?"

"Yes, it was, and thankfully there were no dramas. Except for the play." Dotty smiled.

"It was rather exciting being on stage. I now know why performers talk about the adrenaline rush of being in front of an audience. But I'm pleased I didn't have to speak. I think I'd clam up."

"On stage? What do you mean? I thought you'd just gone to watch something."

"Oh no. Morag, the policewoman Gail in your team introduced me to, asked if I'd take a non-speaking role in the play Dad and I watched on Friday."

"You went back there? After what happened?"

"It's OK, Mum." Dotty laid a reassuring hand on her arm. "Morag was patrolling and anyway, everyone's very nice."

"But one of them murdered Iona McDuff!" Karen's eyes widened with concern.

"What's that woman done now?" slurred Euan, leaning against the doorframe of his and Karen's bedroom.

Karen's nose twitched as she remarked, "He's been up at the Ensign Ewart with his old military buddies."

"The young'uns don't know what it was like back in my day. Bleating on about serving a greater Scotland. Our allegiance is to our monarch. Always has been, and always should be."

"Not that again," muttered Karen. "I hope you didn't cause any trouble," she admonished Euan. "You've never been any good at keeping your mouth closed after a few pints, and you're even worse with a couple of whiskys inside you."

"Dinnae fret, woman. I only said what the rest of my mates were thinking."

He slumped to the floor.

Karen sighed and strode towards him.

Dotty followed, but her mother said, "Go to bed. I'll deal with your father. I'm used to it. He'll be fine in the morning, apart from a sore head."

The next morning, Dotty was woken by banging on the front door. It was half-past eight and Karen must already have left for work.

She pulled herself out of bed and tugged a jumper over her head as she padded to the front door. Earl Grey ignored her, his head in his food bowl. Silently, Dotty thanked her mum for feeding him.

"OK, OK, I'm coming," Dotty called as she fiddled with the spare set of house keys Karen had given her. Finding the right one, she unlocked the front door.

A bald man with a neat grey beard and black-framed glasses stared at her. His lips were pressed together and Dotty immediately tensed. Something was wrong.

Morag stepped out from behind the man and gave Dotty a sympathetic smile.

"Is Euan Abercrombie here?" demanded the man. He was dressed in a light grey suit and a yellow tie which didn't match his current demeanour.

"I think he's still in bed. He was out with his friends last night," Dotty apologised.

"So I hear," replied the man, a steely look in his eyes. "We need him to accompany us to the station."

"What? Why?" exclaimed Dotty, suddenly aware that she was standing on the doorstep in her pyjamas.

"To help us with our enquiries."

"Enquiries into what?"

"I'm not at liberty to say."

It was clear the man wasn't going to give Dotty any information. "And you are?" she asked.

"Inspector Munro." He didn't offer any ID. "I believe you're already acquainted with Sergeant Elliot."

Morag smiled apologetically at Dotty.

"You better come in then."

Dotty was right. Her father was still asleep. She shook him and said, "Dad, wake up. The police are here."

"What?"

"I don't know what they want, but they've made it clear they're not leaving until you've spoken to them." Dotty looked at him. "Grab a shower while I stall them. And clean your teeth, thoroughly."

"I'm not …" began Euan.

"Please, Dad, don't make a scene. I'm sure this is just a misunderstanding."

Dotty returned to the living area. Inspector Munro was still standing by the door leading to the entrance hall while Morag wandered around the living space.

"How long have your parents been here?" Morag asked.

"Less than a year. They moved from Stirling to be closer to my mum's work."

"Gail said she deserved the promotion, but everyone was surprised. The bank is still a man's world."

Inspector Munro grunted.

"Dad's just getting dressed. Can I make you a tea or coffee while you wait?" offered Dotty.

"I'd love a cup of tea," Morag replied.

Dotty entered the kitchen area. Earl Grey was sitting in front of the inspector, staring up at him. Inspector Munro stared back. Who's going to win this battle of wills Dotty wondered as she switched the kettle on.

She felt Earl Grey rub against her legs and heard the inspector grunt again. A man of few words, Dotty decided.

Dotty and Morag stood beside the French windows sipping their tea. "Looks like a better day," Morag observed, trying to sound cheerful.

"That depends," replied Dotty, but as she was about to ask Morag why she was at the flat, her friend shook her head.

Instead, Morag asked, "What time are you needed at the Pleasance this evening?"

"Half past four."

"Do you mind looking after Davy if I drop him off? He's so excited about the play and it'll give my mum a break."

"Sure and perhaps we can …"

"Have a quick drink after the performance. Absolutely."

Euan appeared from his bedroom wearing a pair of creased brown chinos and a khaki-coloured polo shirt. "I'm here. What's this about?"

"Sir, please come with us to the station," said Inspector Munro, stepping forward.

Euan hesitated, but then his shoulders slumped.

"I'll come with you," said Dotty, crossing the living room.

"That won't be necessary," replied the inspector as he led Euan out of the kitchen.

"Well at least tell me where you're taking my father," cried Dotty, annoyed that the Inspector was stonewalling her.

As Morag passed Dotty, she whispered, "St Leonard's Street."

CHAPTER NINETEEN

The first thing Dotty did after her dad was taken away for questioning by Inspector Munro was to call her mum.

"Good morning, Karen Abercrombie's phone. This is Gail speaking."

"Gail. Hi. It's Dotty."

"Are you calling about your dad?"

"Yes, how did you know?"

Gail lowered her voice and whispered, "Morag sent me a message. Has Inspector Munro already left with him?"

"Yes, and Morag said they were going to St Leonard's Street."

"Och, that's on the south side of Edinburgh. I've been waiting for your mum's meeting to finish. She's in with the directors, but I think I'll have to interrupt them. When the police ask you to come to the station voluntarily, it doesn't mean an interview with tea and biscuits. My brother found that out the hard way."

Dotty thought of her dad, and his hangover. How would he act when the police started questioning him?

"Do you think he needs a solicitor?"

"I do, and that's what I want to discuss with your mum. Leave it with me."

Dotty finished the call, relieved that Gail and her mum were doing something to help her dad, but feeling helpless that she wasn't. But then, what could she do in her pyjamas?

After showering and changing, she grabbed half a cup of tea and looked up St Leonard's Street. As Gail had said, it lay to the south of the city, not far from Holyrood Park, which was home to Arthur's Seat, an ancient volcano which tourists climbed hoping for a view of the whole of Edinburgh.

"Meow."

Dotty bent down and stroked Earl Grey. "I'm sorry I'm going out again. But I can't leave Dad on his own at the police station. It wasn't that long ago I was arrested and questioned, and it's an unnerving experience, especially for a proud ex-soldier."

Dotty searched for her bag and the spare house keys, which she found on the kitchen table, remembering when she was arrested for a crime she didn't commit.

Protesting her innocence to police officers who were convinced she was guilty was frustrating and, after a while, depressing. She had felt her integrity and honesty being brought into question.

Earl Grey rubbed against her legs.

"I must stop thinking about my own bad experiences with the police and help Dad," she told her silent cat. "After all, I did prove my innocence by catching the real culprit."

Dotty locked the flat and walked up Broughton Street, where she hailed a taxi for St Leonards police station.

The police station was a modern fawn-brick building which blended in with the residential flats, both old and new, surrounding it.

Only the jarring blue frames of the double height entrance windows, and those in the triangular roof feature, together with large Police Scotland signs, set it apart as a government building.

Dotty entered through the revolving, blue-framed doors, feeling less confident with every step. The blue theme continued inside, with a row of blue metal chairs bolted to the floor along one wall and a blue framed screen separating the receptionist from the public.

Dotty hesitated, standing in the middle of the impersonal space, until she recognised a barked, "Be quiet, Toby."

It was Willow. And he was somewhere to her left.

She turned away from the reception desk and found a small waiting room where Willow, Toby Mills and Jenny Church were sitting.

"Have you been asked to attend a voluntary interview too?" asked Willow, looking up at her and emphasising the word 'voluntary'.

"Not exactly," replied Dotty, stepping inside the room. "But my dad was taken away earlier for questioning."

"Really?" Jenny said in a disbelieving voice as she leaned forward. She was sitting next to Willow.

Toby was sitting on one of the chairs beside the end wall and he crossed his arms as he muttered, "Then maybe we can all leave."

Dotty sat down on the edge of a blue metal seat opposite Willow and Jenny. "I do hope he's OK."

Jenny leaned further forward and placed a hand on Dotty's leg. "I'm sure he will be. After all, what reason would he have to harm Iona McDuff?"

"Hopefully more than we do," quipped Toby.

"Enough," cautioned Willow. "If we've all been hauled in here for questioning, it means the police don't have a primary suspect, and are still looking for one. But in any case, I've called the solicitors my friend recommended and they're sending someone to deal with the situation."

Jenny stared at Toby and jibed, "You could always remain silent. But that would be a first."

Toby frowned and turned away from her.

"But don't the police presume you're guilty if you refuse to say anything or just answer with no comment?" asked Dotty.

"Actually," replied Willow. "It can help you. People are more likely to incriminate themselves, even inadvertently, if they feel they need to speak and 'be helpful'. Far better to say nothing and let the police build a case against them."

"But have you ever tried continuously answering questions with no comment?" asked Jenny. "I did it as a role-playing exercise and it's really hard. Our natural response is to try to make others see that we didn't do anything wrong."

"But if you have?" prompted Toby.

"I wouldn't know," Jenny shot back.

"Children," said Willow, sounding bored.

After a minute or so of silence, Jenny asked, "Why do the police think your father was involved?"

"I'm not sure," replied Dotty. "I think he has some strong views against an independent Scotland because of his career in the military, but not enough to kill someone." The idea was both ridiculous and frightening. "But he was standing next to Iona McDuff when the lights went out."

"Oh, was he?" queried Willow.

Dotty stared at him. "But not when the lights were turned back on. What happened when the lights were off? Why did you and Iona move places?"

"Yes, Willow. Why did you?" pressed Toby, an insolent tone to his voice.

"The answer's pretty straightforward," explained Willow.

"I heard someone cry out in distress and then felt a hand urgently push me along the bench. I had no idea who it was, but instinctively, I moved. Then there was a loud bang, the shot I presume, and the lights came back on. And it was Iona who'd wanted me to move, and she was dead."

"Not necessarily," retorted Toby. "The killer could have pushed you out of the way and deposited Iona's body onto the empty seat. Which I guess is why they're questioning your dad, since he was standing next to her."

"But the shot was after someone wanted Willow to move," argued Jenny.

"That's what he remembers, but someone could have pushed him out of the way, shot Iona and then dumped her body. Besides, there were two shots."

"Were there?" Jenny's voice rose in surprise.

"Yes, I heard two," Dotty confirmed.

"I only remember the one," admitted Willow.

"As it was so dark, I can't see how anyone could have moved Willow, shot Iona, and then sat her body down on the seat. Not unless they had night vision goggles."

"I agree," said Willow. "And for someone like Dotty's father, who didn't know when the lights would be turned off and on, it would be quite a shock. They'd need time to adjust."

"That's right!" exclaimed Dotty. "Dad had no idea what was going to happen in the play. No idea the stage would suddenly be plunged into darkness. No idea Iona McDuff was going to be there. We weren't even invited to the performance."

"You weren't?" chorused Willow, Toby, and Jenny in unison.

Blushing, Dotty admitted, "The tickets were sent to the previous occupants of my parents' flat. It was a last-minute decision to attend."

"Well if your dad didn't do it, this isn't looking too good for us," moaned Toby. "And where is Robbie? He was sitting opposite the victim."

"He said he'd meet us here. That he had some business to take care of first."

"I bet he did," grumbled Toby. "Like hiding the murder weapon."

CHAPTER TWENTY

There was silence in the small waiting room at St Leonard's police station.

A petite lady with a hooked nose and short greying hair appeared in the doorway.

"Lord Thorpe," she asked in a deferential tone, with the trace of an American accent.

"That's me. But please, call me Willow."

Formally the woman replied, "Lord Thorpe. I've been sent to represent you and your colleagues." She looked at Dotty and, wrinkling her nose, declared, "You're not Robert Campbell." Dotty presumed she recognised Toby and Jenny.

"He's not here yet," replied Willow.

"I'm waiting for someone else," admitted Dotty.

"Well. I …" began the solicitor.

"You can speak in front of Dotty. She's one of the cast this week," insisted Willow.

"Very well. I had discussions with various members of the investigating team until the officer in charge finally admitted he has no firm evidence against any of you. So, in my opinion, no reason to inconvenience you by making you wait here to be interviewed. I have agreed that each of you will sign a written statement, which I shall prepare, stating your relationship, if any, with the victim, and your account of Friday evening's events."

"But I've already told the policewoman who's hanging around the theatre all that," complained Toby.

"If you'd prefer to stay ..."

Toby sat up. "No, no. I'll make a statement. But does it have to be here?"

"No, it doesn't, and I suggest we return to your hotel, away from prying ears." The woman stared at Dotty.

"Best idea I've heard all day." Toby jumped to his feet.

As Toby, Willow and Jenny followed the solicitor out of the waiting room, Jenny stopped and asked, "Will you be OK?"

Dotty nodded.

"See you this evening?"

Dotty slowly smiled. "Yes. I'll be there." And she hoped she would be, but what about her dad?

She left the waiting room and joined a queue of people waiting in front of the reception desk. Time dragged on as a woman insisted the police issue country wide alerts for her missing cat. When Dotty's turn finally came, she asked, "I'm here to see Euan Abercrombie."

The receptionist tapped a keyboard. "His solicitor is with him. Are you next of kin?"

"Daughter," replied Dotty politely.

"I'm afraid there isn't anything I can tell you." Dotty started to turn away but stopped and turned back to the receptionist, asking, "Can you tell PC Morag Elliot that Dotty Sayers is in the waiting room?"

The receptionist wrinkled her brow, but she picked up a phone handset and spoke into it.

Dotty returned to the empty waiting room. When the other cast members had been there, it had been bearable, but now, as she sat on her own, she started to feel guilty. If she hadn't insisted she and her dad use the VIP tickets, tickets which were never meant for them, her dad wouldn't be in a police interview room. And what would happen if he was arrested?

"Hi, I've brought you a cup of tea," said a cheerful Morag as she entered the waiting room. "Sitting in here, not knowing what's going on, is the worst, isn't it?" She started nibbling on a biscuit.

"Oops. Sorry. I brought that for you, too. Here's your tea," she said in an apologetic tone.

"Is Dad OK?" enquired Dotty.

"He is now. At first, he was rather difficult. He made it clear he didn't appreciate being dragged out of bed to be interviewed about a murder he knew nothing about. And then he seemed to gain control of himself and refused to say anything. Luckily, a solicitor arrived, and he's with him now, as the interview continues."

"But why question him at all?"

"Because we're under loads of pressure to solve this one. A high-profile victim, at the Fringe. Not that it stopped people coming to the play last night. But there are those who want it dealt with swiftly, and without a fuss."

"And my dad?"

"An easy target, especially as he was overheard last night complaining about plans for an independent Scottish military." Morag sat down next to Dotty.

"But he didn't even want to watch the play. He only went because I persuaded him to, and I wouldn't have done that if I'd known we'd have to go on stage. It's not really my thing. Besides, the tickets weren't even meant for us." Dotty knew she sounded desperate. She sipped her tea, trying to calm down.

"I hear you," agreed Morag. "It's perfectly clear to me your dad had no idea what was going on in the play. And that he hadn't wanted to stand next to the victim, but was forced to when he couldn't find another space. Hopefully, his solicitor will explain all that during the interview."

Dotty was silent, thinking first about her dad, and then about the earlier conversation with Willow, Toby, and Jenny.

"I'll leave you in peace," said Morag, standing up.

"Actually, there is something," said Dotty, gathering her thoughts. "Earlier, we were discussing why Willow moved seats."

"Because Iona pushed him."

"But nobody knows that. It could have been the killer that urged him to move so they could place the body on the seat."

"We have considered that, but it seems rather unnecessary. And there wasn't much time. Besides, there is some doubt when the shot that killed Ms McDuff was fired. Before or after she sat down."

"There is another explanation," said Dotty slowly.

"What?"

"That she wasn't the intended victim."

"Come on!" exclaimed Morag. "Who would have wanted any of the others dead? Don't answer that. I've found a few, mostly men, who would be happy to see the back of Toby Mills."

"Toby wasn't near the victim."

"I know. I was only joking."

"But Willow was. He was supposed to be sitting in the place where Iona McDuff was found dead."

Morag was silent. The smile dissolving.

Then she said, "Lords probably have plenty of enemies. Especially those who are vocal about their political views. But that would mean looking at the case from a completely different angle."

"It would," agreed Dotty.

Morag sat back down.

Dotty didn't interrupt the silence.

Finally, Morag said, "I don't think my superiors will agree with you. They're convinced the intended victim was Ms McDuff. And as they're under huge pressure, they're unlikely to dilute resources and start looking at Lord Thorpe as a target. Indeed, if you take that angle, anyone in the carriage could have been the intended victim."

"Not exactly," argued Dotty. "Although I agree that those, like my father or Robbie Campbell, who were near Iona would fall into that category."

Morag stood up and laid a hand on Dotty's shoulder. "I hear where you're coming from, but you and me, we don't have the power to influence this investigation. I'm just a foot soldier and you're …"

Dotty smiled, "I'm an interfering busybody. I've been called that before, but it didn't stop me being right and catching the culprit."

Morag removed her hand and stepped back. "All right. You are at the theatre, after all. See if anyone says or does anything to back up your theory, but don't interfere with the official case, and don't put yourself in danger. One murder in the theatre is quite enough."

CHAPTER TWENTY-ONE

Morag left Dotty alone in the police waiting room.

Ten minutes later, a breathless Karen rushed in. "Hi. Is your dad still being questioned?" She took a breath and continued, "And do you know if the solicitor I organised has turned up?"

"Hi Mum, I haven't seen dad. But my friend Morag told me he does have a solicitor with him in the interview room. I've been waiting here since I arrived."

"The receptionist told me to wait, too. But for how long?"

Dotty wondered why Karen was asking her. Admittedly, she knew of the inner workings of Cirencester police station, but Karen didn't know that, and this was a large Scottish station. They might do things differently here.

"Dad hasn't actually been arrested, but in this interview the police will be trying to gather enough evidence, or probable cause, to apprehend him for killing Iona McDuff."

"But that's ridiculous. Why would he?" Karen dragged her hands through her sleek shoulder length hair.

"Because the police are under pressure to arrest someone. Anyone, I guess, and he was standing next to the victim when the incident happened. And apparently last night he was rather vocal with his views on Scottish independence."

"I knew last night was a bad idea, meeting up with his old military mates. But I didn't expect him to be arrested." Karen strode down the small room, turned on her heels and paced back.

"He might not be. Members of the cast from the play were also brought in for questioning, but their solicitor is organising for each of them to give a statement instead of being interviewed."

"Why couldn't Euan do that?" Karen continued to pace the room.

"Because it happened so quickly, and we didn't have a lawyer to hand. But don't worry, it means the police aren't pursuing him as their sole suspect."

"But he is the easiest target. I should have got here earlier." Karen's phone rang.

"Yes," she answered impatiently. "No, you'll have to start the presentation without me." And then after a short response from the other party, "It's only internal."

Karen finished the call and stopped in front of Dotty. "How long do we have to wait?" She was clearly under pressure to return to work.

"I've no idea. Police interviews can be drawn out as they check leads, and try to find reasons to detain a suspect." Dotty knew her tone was sour, but she remembered her own experience when she'd been left in an interview room for most of the morning while the police came in and out.

"Why are you so bitter about the police?" asked Karen.

Dotty dropped her gaze to her clasped hands, but still felt Karen's gaze on her.

"Have you ever been arrested, Dotty?" pressed Karen.

"Yes," Dotty squeaked.

Karen settled on the seat next to Dotty and, in a surprisingly tender voice, said, "Tell me about it."

Dotty had hardly spoken to her parents since Al died and she'd started her job at Akemans auction house and antiques centre.

Her father had been insistent she return home, but she'd hesitated, feeling he only wanted her to replace Karen as the wife around the house doing the cooking, cleaning, and washing. And their relationship had been strained ever since.

And she'd never been able to open up to Karen, who she'd always felt was reserved and cold towards her. That she was too busy sorting out her own life.

"I'm sorry I wasn't there for you as a child," Karen said in a soft voice.

Had Karen realised why Dotty hadn't answered her? And it was the first time she'd ever apologised.

"What do you remember about your childhood?" pressed her mother.

Dotty considered the question.

"Callum."

"Your brother." Karen smiled nostalgically. "It was so much easier with him. Euan was at home most of the time and the regiment was a family. I was young, and happy, and so proud of my baby boy."

Dotty pressed her lips together but held back from saying, unlike your baby girl.

"And then your dad was promoted and increased responsibility led to more time away on courses and exercises, and then frequent tours of Northern Ireland. They were the worst. I had wanted another baby, but by the time you came along, I'd given up hope and everything was different. Callum's needs as an eight-year-old boy were so different from yours as a baby. And with Euan away, I had the house to run and other wives to support, and it was so full on. I didn't even have a spare hour to go the hairdressers."

Dotty felt something inside her shrivel up. "I knew you never wanted me."

Karen froze. Finally, in a disbelieving voice, she said, "Don't you ever think that. You were this perfect little baby. So content. All you did was smile and gurgle. Everyone wanted to hold you when I had to rush onto the football field to console Callum when he missed a goal, or stop him fighting with a friend over table football. I loved you. You were perfect. Too perfect. I just …" Karen choked ... "couldn't cope."

Couldn't cope! Her mother had always coped. When the girls at school, she had no idea which school, had fought over the doll her father had brought back from somewhere and pulled its arm off, it was her mum who'd glued it back on.

And it was her mum who'd spent hours with her as she'd struggled with her maths in secondary school, as their latest move meant she was over half a year behind. And her mum, who'd shouted down the phone at the military repair service that this was an emergency as water was flooding the kitchen. She'd never not been able to cope.

"I'm sorry I wasn't there for you," apologised Karen again.

But actually, she had been. When Dotty had been younger, and her dad was away. The house was always tidy, and she'd insisted on cooking meals with fresh ingredients as they were growing children.

When had that stopped? Dotty wasn't sure. But there had come a point, after one house move, when her mum no longer did everything for her.

"I know you resented my job with the estate agent, and I felt awful dragging you to viewings after school, so you'd have to finish your homework in the car, but I just needed to do something. Something on my own. For myself. And earning my own money was liberating."

Dotty could see that, but that was when Karen had abandoned her.

"And when your dad stepped in and offered to take you to netball practice, and swimming lessons, I was delighted. He'd missed so much of your younger years."

Karen leaned back in her chair and sighed.

Dotty sensed there was something else. A but.

"But he took over. Became so protective of you. He just wouldn't let me in. And he even stopped you visiting friends and going to parties. But you adored him. I was torn and, in the end, I concentrated on what I needed to do to get strong, and by the time I could stand up to your father again, he had total control over you. Neither of you would listen to me."

A memory stirred in Dotty's mind. An invitation to a sleepover. Her mother standing in the living room with an overnight bag and her dad stepping between her and Dotty and saying that it wasn't safe for Dotty to go. Who knew what her friends might get up to? Drink. Drugs. Even boys.

Dotty remembered shrinking back. When the arguing had stopped, she'd called out, "It's OK. I don't want to go, anyway." But she had wanted to go, and she remembered her mother's look of disappointment while her father had smiled in satisfaction.

Dotty moved her hand across and laid it on her mother's thigh.

"Mrs Abercrombie? Mrs Sayers?" asked a young, uniformed man, who stood in the waiting room entrance.

"Mr Abercrombie is being released under investigation."

Karen jumped up and asked, "What does that mean?"

Dotty pulled herself to her feet and stood beside her mum, a hand on her arm. "It means they think Dad was involved, but don't have sufficient evidence to charge him." She looked directly at the young police officer and asked, "Is he being processed?"

"Yes, we're currently taking his DNA and fingerprints."

"What? Why?" Karen tensed under Dotty's touch.

"Don't worry, Mum. It's part of the process and it doesn't hurt."

"But he didn't do it. And his details will be on the system now."

"We can ask for them to be removed later, can't we, Constable?"

The young man gulped. "I believe so. If he isn't convicted."

"Karen, Dotty," Euan called.

The young constable stepped out of the way, and Karen rushed across to hug Euan. When she stopped and stepped back, Euan remained frozen to the spot, staring at his wife.

"Come on, let's get you home. Or would you prefer to stop and eat at The Lost Sock Diner?"

Euan's face softened into a grin. "Now I think about it. I'm starving."

CHAPTER TWENTY-TWO

Dotty followed her parents through a laundrette into a small room laid out with tables and chairs.

"This is different," she commented.

"And they do the best breakfast," smiled Euan, as he pulled out a high-backed wooden chair and sat down. "Thank you for waiting for me. And for finding that solicitor." He stared at the large, two-sided laminated menu.

"That's OK," said Karen, sitting opposite Euan, "although Dotty was the one who waited for you all morning. I couldn't get away until after the directors' meeting."

"Of course," replied Euan through pinched lips.

"But Mum organised your solicitor," Dotty insisted, settling herself next to Karen.

Euan dropped his menu to the table. "And without him, I'm certain I'd have been charged. But the young man, give him his dues, argued a very articulate case for my release, albeit under investigation, on the grounds of lack of evidence."

"I presume all they have against you is your proximity to the victim and your outspoken opinion of some of her policies," voiced Dotty.

"That about sums it up. Ah, here comes the waiter. A pint of Tennents," Euan requested.

Dotty felt her mother tense, but she refrained from saying anything about Euan's choice of drink. Dotty ordered a pot of breakfast tea and Karen a double espresso.

"But what about the murder weapon? You didn't smuggle a gun into the performance, did you?" asked Karen.

"Don't be ridiculous," Euan bridled.

"They haven't found the murder weapon yet," Dotty revealed.

"Well I wish they'd hurry up. Then maybe I can clear my name," grumbled Euan.

The waiter brought their drinks and asked, "Are you ready to order?"

"Just give us a few minutes, chief," replied Euan, picking up the menu again.

Karen turned to Dotty and said, "I recommend the All Day breakfast, the eggs Florentine or the burgers." She grinned at Dotty. "I'm going for a burger," which was unlike Karen, who usually stuck to salads.

Dotty looked at the menu. "I'll join you. The one with bacon and avocado."

Having spent a leisurely lunch with her parents, Dotty returned to the flat with her father.

She'd expected her mother to rush back to work, but in the end, she told Karen to go to the office and she'd settle her dad at home before heading to the Pleasance for the evening show.

In the back of the taxi, on the way to the Pleasance, Dotty sent Karen a message.

Dad at home watching football. Pasta bake ready to go. 30 mins in the oven. Salad in the fridge. I'll be back around 9.

Dotty walked into the Pleasance Side Theatre at five past five. The students were gathered in small groups at the edge of the stage, and Skye was in her control booth.

When Skye saw Dotty, she bent down and then straightened up, holding a black police jacket.

"Let's see if this fits," she said, descending from her control booth to meet Dotty at the bottom of the steps.

Shrugging off her raincoat, Dotty slipped the jacket over the black t-shirt she was wearing. She'd borrowed it from Karen for the performance, together with a pair of tailored black trousers.

Neither she nor Karen owned a 1950s style skirt, and Dotty only needed to symbolise that she was a police officer, not be dressed in the full attire.

As Dotty buttoned up the front of the jacket, Skye ran her hand over the shoulders and down the back. Finally, she stood in front of Dotty, appraising her. "Perfect."

"That looks great," enthused a breathless Jenny as she joined them.

"Sorry I'm late. We've been sitting with a pedantic solicitor all afternoon while she prepared our statements for the police. Luckily, she let me leave, but Willow, Toby and Robbie are still with her." Jenny glanced at her watch. "I hope they get here in time."

"Is there anything you want to go over?" asked Skye.

"Maybe a few scenes with Dotty. Now she's dressed the part," grinned Jenny.

With only the two of them on stage, and with nothing else to do, Jenny helped Dotty, showing her where and how to stand, and what to do when the action was taking place elsewhere.

Jenny reminded her to remember her feet, and that they were grounded to the stage; to focus on her breathing; and if she felt she was starting to panic, to concentrate on one of the props she was holding.

Dotty certainly felt more at ease by the time the rest of the cast arrived, entering through the emergency exit door.

"Twenty minutes until curtain-up," called Robbie as he rushed up the steps onto the stage. Everyone get dressed and take your positions." He hurried across the stage, looking across at Skye.

Was that Davy standing beside her? Dotty hadn't seen him or Morag arrive.

"Any problems?" asked Robbie.

Skye shook her head.

Dotty remained by her peg as Jenny helped Willow fasten the buttons on his shirt and Toby cursed as he pulled on his trousers.

"Where have they been?" asked Sheena, the play's victim, as she sidled up to Dotty. "Enjoying a leisurely lunch?"

"We were all at the police station this morning," Dotty revealed.

Sheena's brow furrowed. "Why? And what have you done?"

"I was there for my father. The police questioned him again about Iona McDuff"s death."

"And how did that go?"

"They released him, but he's still under investigation. As, I suspect, are the members of the theatre group, although they got away with only providing written statements."

"Do you think I'll be questioned again?" Sheena appeared excited by the prospect rather than apprehensive.

"I think we all will be."

"Two minutes," called Robbie. "Take your places."

The chatter amongst the audience subsided as the 1950s music started and the performance began.

In the second act, Dotty realised she didn't have the handcuffs. Feeling her face flush and her heart start to race she saw Davy at the side of the stage madly waving at her and holding up the handcuffs.

She made her way across to him as calmly as she could, trying her best not to interrupt Toby and Jenny, who were engaged in a heated discussion. Leaning down, she whispered, "Thank you," but as she stood back up, she hit her head on the side of the sandbag.

"Ow …" she cried but quickly clamped her hand over her mouth.

Davy tilted his head as he looked at her with concern.

"I'm OK," she mouthed, but rubbed the area above her right eye where she'd collided with the sandbag, and more particularly with something inside it.

Dotty tried to concentrate on the remainder of the play, but she was preoccupied with the sandbag and the object hiding in it. An object with a solid edge. She was relieved when the play was over but frustrated by Morag's absence.

The theatre was nearly empty when Morag finally appeared, with Davy by her side. "Davy said you had a disagreement with one of the sandbags. Are you OK?"

"I think so." Dotty turned her head towards Morag, who peered at it.

"You've a nasty bruise. Let's hope it doesn't reach your eye. But I'm surprised you got that just from a sandbag."

Dotty hissed, "That's why I've been waiting for you. I don't think it is just a sandbag. Come on. I want to look inside it."

"This is the one." Davy pointed excitedly to a faded green canvas bag.

Morag pulled on it and a scraping noise came from the roof of the theatre.

"Gonnae no' dae that!" cried Robbie, rushing across the stage to them. He'd been organising the removal of the makeshift carriage and, despite his baffling Scottish phrase, it was clear to Dotty he wanted Morag to stop.

"I need to look inside this bag," Morag stated.

"Why?" Robbie wrinkled his nose.

"We'll see why when I do," replied Morag with an authoritative tone.

Dotty hoped she was right and that all the fuss was justified.

Robbie called across to the students. "Come and help me with this."

The students put down whatever they were carrying and crowded round Robbie.

"This is going to be tricky. We need to remove this weight," he indicated to the sandbag, "without whatever it's holding up in the roof crashing down. So I need you to take its weight and gently lower whatever's up there. And one of you needs to work the pulley."

Robbie continued to instruct the students until a backdrop of the Edinburgh skyline was lowered to the back of the stage and the sandbag was untied and placed on the wooden floorboards.

The students crowded round it and were joined by the cast.

"What's going on?" called Willow, the last to arrive.

"Everyone stand back," instructed Morag in a voice Dotty presumed she used when policing football or rugby matches. She was wearing a pair of blue latex gloves.

Unzipping the top of the canvas bag, she thrust her hand inside and Dotty watched as it searched the contents.

"Got you," grunted Morag in satisfaction.

She pulled her hand out of the bag, clasping the object she'd found.

Davy cried excitedly, "It's a gun!"

CHAPTER TWENTY-THREE

On stage in the Pleasance Side Theatre, the cast of *Underground Murder* all started talking at once.

"Enough," called Morag, but they ignored her.

"Silence!"

Everyone stopped talking.

"Has anyone seen this gun before?" demanded Morag.

Robbie stepped forward. "It's not one of the props. It looks real to me."

"It is real," Morag confirmed.

Davy jumped up and down in delight while some of the students gasped.

"How did it get in the sandbag?" Willow asked.

"That's the million-dollar question," remarked Morag, studying Willow. "My guess is the murderer hid it there."

There was a collective gasp.

"Which means one of you." With a stony expression, Morag surveyed the group.

"Don't look at me," muttered one of the students. "I wasn't even here when it happened."

The other students nodded in agreement.

Morag removed a transparent plastic evidence bag from her pocket.

Dotty stepped forward and opened it so Morag could place the gun inside. It was lighter than she had expected.

"Hopefully there will be fingerprints on it to tell us which of you shot Iona McDuff."

This time, the assembled group remained still and silent. Even Davy seemed to understand the seriousness of the situation.

Robbie cleared his throat. "OK, everyone. Let's reattach the sandbag and hoist the backdrop back up. We don't need everyone, so can some of you finish clearing away the train carriage?"

Morag inclined her head to Dotty, and they moved away from the rest of the crew.

"Well done," praised Morag. "Hopefully, this will be the breakthrough we need in the case. I must say, it's not the usual type of gun I see on the streets of Edinburgh. It's lighter, neater, and more sophisticated."

"I don't think it's the type my father would know about. If he wanted to shoot anyone and needed a gun, he'd go to his military contacts."

"The Glock the army use is much lighter than the old Brownings. Still, this isn't either of them. I'm not sure what make it is." Morag held up the bag and peered at the gun.

"Do you think your colleagues will stop investigating my dad now?"

Morag pinched her lips together. "Not yet. Not without concrete evidence he's innocent."

"But he's the one person who had no idea Iona McDuff would be at the play. He didn't know he'd be at the play," insisted Dotty, knowing her voice sounded shrill.

Morag stepped back. "Hey, I don't disagree, but frankly, until the murderer is caught, everyone is under suspicion. Even me."

Dotty froze. Gathering herself together, she asked, "Really?"

"Oh, yes. I haven't told you about the interviews I've had with the ACC and other senior members of the investigating team. I was a latecomer to the police force. Before I had Davy, I worked at several of the big assurance companies.

"But when he started school, I didn't want to return to a desk job. I saw an advert for community police officers, but I was offered a full-time position. And most of the time, I enjoy it. I doubt I'll ever be promoted, so I do my hours, catch the bad guys, and give Davy a hug at the end of the day."

Dotty smiled. "Good for you."

"But the point is, I'm still an outsider. So while nobody will admit it, I am considered a suspect. But now I'd better deliver this gun to the station before I take Davy home." Morag turned and shouted, "Davy."

Dotty decided it was also time to leave and called "Goodbye" as she left with Morag and Davy through the emergency exit.

"Would you like a lift home?" asked Morag.

"No, thanks. It's out of your way and I can take a taxi."

Back at her parent's flat, Karen was working on her laptop at the kitchen table. There was no sign of Euan and the lights in the living room were off and the evening light fading outside.

Wearily, her mother looked up at her and asked, "Good show?"

"I think so." Dotty peeled off her lightweight raincoat and hung it on the back of a chair. "But I was too preoccupied to take much notice."

Dotty turned to face Karen.

"What have you done? Is that a bruise?" Karen stood and, joining Dotty, brushed her hair away from her face. "I still haven't organised a hair appointment with all that's happened. That's nasty. Let me find the arnica to put on it to reduce the bruising."

As Karen quietly opened her bedroom door, Dotty switched the kettle on.

"Meow."

Dotty reached down and picked up Earl Grey. "You're getting heavier. Is someone feeding you too much?"

Earl Grey appraised her with his large, yellow eyes.

"I know. I haven't been giving you much attention. And the twins aren't here to pet you like they did in France."

The kettle boiled and, guiltily, Dotty placed Earl Grey back down on the oak floor.

"Here we are," said Karen as she returned to the kitchen table.

"Take two of these small tablets now, and again when you wake up. They're herbal, so they won't have any side effects. And let me rub some of this cream on your forehead."

Dotty allowed her mother's gentle fingers to massage the cream into her sore forehead. It was a strange sensation and one she savoured as she sat down with her cup of tea. Love and intimacy weren't feelings she was used to. But every now and again, to feel someone's affection was consoling.

"I put your father to bed early. I'm not sure how many beers he drank this afternoon. But at least I managed to get some of your delicious pasta into him first. Thank you for that."

"No problem," said Dotty, grateful for the calm of the flat. "We found the murder weapon this evening."

"The gun. Where was it?"

Dotty explained how she'd bumped her head on the sandbag and when Morag searched it, she'd found the gun.

"So that'll prove your father wasn't involved."

"I hope so, but Morag wasn't confident that anyone will be beyond suspicion until the real killer is found. But it will depend on whether any fingerprints are found on the gun."

"So tell me, how do you know so much about police procedures and police stations? Were you really arrested?" asked Karen.

Dotty started to tell her mother about Keya, Sergeant Varma, her best friend in the Cotswolds and her boss, Inspector Evans, and how, when she'd started working at Akemans auction house and antiques centre and she'd been entangled in a murder investigation.

As her mother seemed interested, she continued and told her about other cases, and the various antique frauds she'd helped uncover.

Finally, she admitted that some members of the Cirencester Police had thought she was responsible for stealing valuable items and trying to smuggle them out of the country. And then they thought she'd killed someone.

"But there's no way you'd harm anyone. It's not in your nature," defended Karen.

"Thank you," Dotty acknowledged. "And I'm lucky. I had friends with the same view, and they helped me. But in the in the end, we were all surprised by the real culprit. He was one of us and I was very lucky to be rescued when he tried to kill me."

Instinctively, Dotty touched her throat where her scarf had been tightened as the mastermind behind a string of antique frauds and numerous murders realised she'd seen though his charade. She shivered.

"Are you OK?" Karen asked, a note of concern in her voice.

"It wasn't a pleasant experience. But spending the last three months in the south of France has helped."

"And what are you going to do now? Will you return to the Cotswolds? And what about your job? Will you have to find a new one?"

"I think they've found a replacement receptionist, but there's a place for me as a valuer and they need someone to organise the monthly auctions. But I haven't made up my mind about going back. I'm not sure if it's what I want to do."

Karen placed her hand on Dotty's arm. "You're welcome to stay here as long as you like. It's lovely having you around."

Dotty's phone pinged.

"Who's messaging you so late?" asked Karen.

"I'm not sure. Only Morag and Robbie, the play producer, have my number in Edinburgh. I hope it isn't bad news from the Cotswolds." Dotty didn't recognise the number, but she read the message.

Hi, it's Jenny. Robbie gave me your number. We've been invited to a private tour of Edinburgh Castle in the morning before it's open to the public. Toby says it's too early and Robbie's been loads of times before. Do you want to come? And what about your police friend? We're meeting by the entrance at 7.50 am. XXX

"That's nice," said Dotty. "I've been invited by Jenny Church to join the cast for a private tour of the castle tomorrow morning."

"What a great opportunity, especially as it's so busy in the summer. Will you go?"

"Yes, and they have two tickets. Do you think Dad will come with me? I know he must have visited lots of times, but I think doing something together might help us reconnect. I feel we've been drifting apart since I arrived in Edinburgh."

"The trouble with your father is that he doesn't have a purpose in life. And my promotion, and then your job at the antiques centre, means he feels rather useless."

Dotty went to bed with so many thoughts swirling around in her mind. She set her alarm clock and turned off the light as Earl Grey settled on top of the duvet, curling into the small of her back.

"Night night, boy."

CHAPTER TWENTY-FOUR

"Beep, beep. Beep, beep."

Dotty stirred.

"Beep, Beep."

She reached for her phone and squinting at it turned off the alarm. Half-past six. Why had she set her alarm so early?

Earl Grey resisted her attempts to turn over.

Last night. Sitting with her mum. The message from Jenny. She was going to Edinburgh Castle.

She hauled herself out of bed as Earl Grey yawned, stretched, and settled back down. She stroked the top of his head. "That's a great idea, but if I don't get up, I'll miss the visit to Edinburgh Castle."

She showered, dressed, and entered the kitchen, finding Karen eating an apple while she made herself coffee.

"Your dad's in the shower. He resisted the idea of going with you, especially with the theatre group, but I explained it's a large place and you don't have to explore it with everyone else. I also said he could tell you about his military experiences, and that he's as good a tour guide as any in the museums."

Karen lowered her voice, "So even if he is a bit boring, and you've heard his stories before, try to listen and humour him. His time in the army means so much to him. It defines him."

This was as much of a pep talk as Karen had ever given Dotty.

"Ok. Thanks, Mum."

"And now, as I missed much of yesterday, I'm going to the office early. Can you get your dad a cup of coffee and make sure he eats some breakfast before you go?"

Karen left and Dotty made herself a cup of tea and chopped some fruit to sprinkle over her muesli.

Ten minutes later, her father appeared, clean shaven and dressed in chinos and a short-sleeved shirt.

Dotty made him a cup of coffee as he placed two pieces of bread in the toaster.

There was an awkward silence between them.

Eventually, Euan said, "Sorry about the last couple of days. Things have got a bit out of hand."

Dotty wasn't sure how to respond.

"Going out drinking on a Monday evening is never a good way to start the week. But I didn't expect to be hauled into the police station yesterday."

"Morag, my police contact, says we're all still under suspicion, but hopefully finding the gun last night will help clear us."

"Where did they find it?" asked Euan, as his toast popped up.

"It was at the theatre all the time, hidden in a sandbag, hanging at the side of the stage."

Euan buttered his toast. "Very convenient for someone wanting to dispose of it quickly. I presume it is the weapon used to kill Iona McDuff?"

"We'll have to wait for the forensics team to confirm that, and whose, if any, fingerprints are found on it."

Euan carried his plate to the kitchen table. "Well, mine won't be, so it'll be one less reason for the police to call me back to the station. Now, how long until we have to leave?"

Dotty checked her watch. Twenty past seven. "Ten minutes, but we'll need to take a taxi."

Dotty and Euan arrived early at Edinburgh Castle at a quarter to eight. They had easily found a taxi on Broughton Street and the traffic to the old town had been light.

Dotty guessed most of the tourists had been up late the night before or were enjoying leisurely breakfasts in their hotels.

The sky was a pale blue and the sunlight warming. It might be August, but Dotty felt a chill in the air as she stood by the gates to the castle.

"Those are the seats for the Tattoo," said Euan, indicating to the temporary stands on the other side of the entrance gate. They rose up and blocked out any view of the castle.

"Wow, a lot of people must watch it."

"Over 200,000 people every year and it's always sold out. I haven't been able to find us tickets yet."

"Hi there," called Jenny, rubbing her hands together as she joined them. Willow, who seemed to be struggling for breath, followed her, with other groups of people behind them.

Jenny held her hand out to Euan. "Jenny Church. I think you were at the performance last Friday, but we didn't get a chance to meet."

"Euan Abercrombie, formerly of the Royal Regiment of Scotland."

Willow stopped, took several breaths as he looked across at Euan. "A military man. Just the person we need for a tour of the castle. Is it still used as an army base?"

"Only for administrative and ceremonial purposes, and to oversee the museums. But out of hours, the regiment still provides sentries. Checking on them at three o'clock in the morning is one of a young officer's most annoying jobs."

"I should think so," said Jenny. "You wouldn't get me out of bed to do it."

"Is everyone ready?" called a rich feminine voice with a strong Scottish accent.

"How wonderful," whispered Jenny. "A guide from the Scottish isles."

Their guide did embrace Scottish traditions and, despite it being summer, she was wearing a tailored green jacket with a red and green tartan scarf and a thistle-shaped brooch. Above her practical black lace-up shoes, she wore tights and a green and red tartan wool skirt.

"Follow me," the guide instructed her flock, and they fell in behind her obediently.

"I've had enough of hills," panted Willow.

"Not too much further to the top," Euan assured him. After passing the back of the Tattoo stands, they entered Edinburgh Castle through a stone archway set in the high stone walls.

The solid walls funnelled them up a cobbled road to a second stone archway, after which they came out at the battlements which protected the castle from an invasion from the east.

Dotty wanted to stop to admire the view, but she was carried along with the rest of the group as they continued in an anti-clockwise climb taking them past a row of Neo-classical looking buildings, and on past St Margaret's Chapel, which their guide told them was the oldest building in the complex.

Finally, they reached a courtyard at the top of the castle complex.

"This is Crown Square," announced their guide. She wasn't the least bit out of breath.

Dotty was puffing, and Willow was doubled over, resting his hands on his thighs. Even Euan was breathing heavily.

"The first exhibit we'll see today is our Crown Jewels, the oldest in Great Britain. The sceptre and sword of state are made of gold, silver, and precious gems, and the crown was designed for James V, who first wore it in 1540."

Their guide stopped so the significance of her words could sink in.

"But what you might think looks out of place in the display is the large piece of stone. This is the Stone of Destiny. Although its origins are unknown, geologists have estimated it's over 400 million years old. It was used for the inauguration of Scottish monarchs until it was stolen from Scone Abbey in 1296 by Edward I of England. He had it built into a throne in Westminster Abbey which has been used by English kings and queens during their coronations ever since."

"Didn't someone steal it?" called a voice from amongst the group.

"Four students, on Christmas Day in 1950."

"And what about the suffragettes?" asked Jenny.

"They did target the stone, but their bomb damaged the chair which held it, not the stone itself."

"It's had a colourful history," whispered Willow. "I bet it's not the original."

Dotty didn't think the guide heard him, but she said in a voice of cast-iron certainty. "This is the original stone."

Willow raised his eyebrows.

The group filed into the small room holding the Crown Jewels and, after walking around the glass display box admiring them, they moved on to the state rooms, which displayed gilt-framed portraits beneath ornate plaster ceilings.

Jenny was peering into a side room. When Dotty joined her, she said, "This is the room where Mary Queen of Scots gave birth to James I of England and James VI of Scotland. She might have had her differences with the English Queen Elizabeth, but her son united the English and Scottish nations."

Dotty noticed the crest on the wall above the wooden panelling with two rearing white unicorns.

As they wandered around the staterooms, she asked Jenny, "Have you been to Edinburgh before?"

"Several times as a child and as a teen. My parents preferred holidays in Scotland, rather than abroad. And we performed at the festival for nearly ten years, but I haven't been back since then. It was karma that Willow should decide to run his play here the year my stand-up show finally got accepted."

"How many years have you been rejected?"

Jenny laughed. "Ten. But that's because for the first six, I was pretty rubbish. You see, Toby and I both started with Willow and his theatre group. I was twenty-six and already bored with my work in recruitment. I'd made loads of money in London but spent most of it and was completely burned out.

"I joined a smaller agency in Cheltenham, hoping to get some balance in my life, and one of my colleagues said they were auditioning for a part in a play. I went along with him and was amazed when Willow offered me the role of the police inspector."

"The one you're playing this time?"

"Yes, and I still fit into the uniform." Jenny smiled proudly.

They both stared at two huge paintings of a man and woman, both wearing black, with white Jacobean style ruffles around their necks.

"Did you give up your job?"

"Gosh, no. The play was well received in Edinburgh, but Toby was the star. He received several offers from TV shows and finally accepted the one for a part in a new soap opera, *Driftwood Cove*. He and the show have done very well over the years. He's a household name now."

"And you?"

"I went back to work but continued to be part of Willow's theatre group. We put on several shows a year and, as I said, continued to take one to the Edinburgh Festival each summer."

"Were you jealous of Toby?" It was the question she'd been dying to ask, but she hadn't meant to be so blunt.

They wandered out of the staterooms back into the courtyard.

"Not really. Sure, I'd have loved to have been offered a part in a TV show, but I knew they weren't handed out to everyone. And then the same friend who'd suggested I audition for Willow's theatre group, dared me to stand up on stage at a local comedy club. I think he wanted to get me back for always playing practical jokes in the office. Recruitment work can be rather dull," Jenny confided.

Willow strode up to them and declared, "What a knowledgeable man your father is, Dotty. He told me all about the different regiments remembered in the Scottish War Memorial. Do you know, one in five Scottish soldiers who enlisted in World War I never made it home?"

Dotty was surprised it wasn't more.

"Have you been in the Great Hall yet?" asked Willow enthusiastically.

Jenny and Dotty shook their heads and followed Euan and Willow across the cobbled courtyard.

Dotty heard their guide announce, "This is the Great Hall, completed in 1511 for King James IV."

She turned to Jenny and asked, "Weren't you terrified standing on stage trying to make people laugh?"

"Terrified? I loved it. And even more so when people didn't laugh. I found I started making fun of them and the rest of the audience thought that was hilarious. And that's OK for comedy clubs and smaller venues, but to perform on larger stages you need a proper show and that's taken me years of practice to perfect."

They stood in the centre of the wooden beamed hall, with displays of weapons and suits of armour exhibited around its perimeter.

"You're still young," Jenny said to Dotty, "but I think I needed the experiences of life, of being an unmarried, childless woman moving into the period of life when I can no longer have children, to find the meaning I needed for my shows and to be able to connect to an audience."

"It must have been frustrating having a show you knew was good enough for the Fringe Festival, but it was still rejected."

"Oliver Cromwell's army captured the castle in 1650 and they turned The Great Hall into a barracks for over three hundred soldiers," explained their guide.

Jenny and Dotty wandered out of The Great Hall.

"It was frustrating watching other comedians launch their shows from the festival, but I kept performing on the smaller stages and continuing to work my way up."

Jenny sounded as if she'd accepted her exclusion from the festival without holding any grudges. But what did others feel about Jenny?

Dotty stopped and asked, "Do you think you've made any enemies during that time? Anyone who would want to kill you?"

"Kill me? Don't be so ridiculous. Why would you even think that?"

"Because I'm not convinced Iona McDuff was the intended victim."

"But I wasn't on stage," protested Jenny.

Holding eye contact with the stand-up comedian, Dotty said in a slow, calm voice, "I know."

Jenny stepped back and knocked into a woman taking a photograph.

"Sorry," she apologised, before hissing, "You think I killed Iona?"

Dotty dropped her arms to her side and in an apologetic tone said, "As you said, you weren't on stage, so you had the opportunity. But no, I don't think you killed Iona, but you might have seen the person who did."

CHAPTER TWENTY-FIVE

Dotty followed Jenny out of the courtyard at the top of the castle and down to the next level, where she climbed some stone steps. But instead of stopping beside the gigantic cannon on display, she entered St Margaret's Chapel.

In the curved bay at the end of the single-roomed stone building, an altar was shrouded with a turquoise cover and an altar cloth embroidered with a simple cross intertwined with white flowers.

Jenny didn't look up when Dotty stopped beside her as they both considered the altar, but said, "I was in the wings at the back of the stage, and I did see movement towards the front. I've been wracking my brains trying to remember who and what I saw, but it was all a blur. I remember seeing the flash of the gun."

"But not who was holding it?"

Jenny bowed her head. "I'm afraid not."

As they exited the chapel, Dotty continued to question Jenny, aware that she might be pushing her luck. "You know the cast. Would anyone on stage have a reason to kill anyone else? In particular, those near Iona, such as Willow, whose seat she was found in, or Robbie, who was sitting opposite her?"

"I don't know Robbie. Willow hired him specifically for the play. He's a local boy and has produced several Fringe productions. He wasn't supposed to be acting, but Sebastian, whose role he's taken over, was called away to film abroad. Lucky thing."

They moved across to the ramparts and for a moment just took in the panoramic view.

Jenny continued, "I've known Willow a long time, and he's certainly forthright in his views. And not everyone agrees that peers, by courtesy of their birthright, should still have a say in how our country is run. And that is probably a popular viewpoint in Scotland."

Jenny tapped the stone battlements before asking, "If Willow was the intended target, could he still be in danger?"

It wasn't a question Dotty had considered. "I suppose he could. Do you think we should tell him?"

"No, he'd only brush it away and say we're mistaken."

Dotty watched as, far below, a blue-roofed train slowly progressed westwards along the tracks between her and Edinburgh's new town.

"But I should keep an eye on him," reflected Jenny. She stepped away from the battlements and said, "And now I feel like a cup of coffee."

They descended the stone steps and followed the cobbled road until they met Willow and Euan. "That was fascinating, Euan, but I need a break. Can I buy you a drink?" asked Willow.

"We're heading to the cafe too," Dotty said.

The cafe was on the lower level and inside it had a wonderful display of cakes, traybakes, and pastries. Somehow, they each ended up with something sweet to eat, along with their teas and coffees.

Carrying them outside, they found an empty picnic table and sat down. Guiltily, Dotty observed her chocolate chip muffin.

"Don't worry, your mum's not here," joked Euan, who was sitting opposite her.

Willow bit into an individual round pastry case. "Curd tart. I haven't had one of these in years. But what's wrong with you, Jenny? You're uncharacteristically quiet and introspective."

Jenny was silently staring at her phone. She placed it on the wooden table and said, "Sorry, it's just the discussion Dotty and I have been having."

"About the castle?"

"No, about the incident on Friday. Dotty's not convinced Iona

McDuff was the intended victim, which means the killer might try again."

"And kill who?" asked Willow, brushing pastry crumbs off his lips.

"Robbie, or, more likely, you."

"Don't be ridiculous. Who would want to kill me?"

"See what I mean?" Jenny said, looking at Dotty.

"It is a fair point," Euan said, considering the idea. "After all, Iona McDuff was found in your seat, and as a peer of the realm, you'll have plenty of people who don't like what you stand for. And one of them could be a fanatic who's decided to make an example of you."

"Like some sort of martyr?" suggested Willow. "But the only people on stage were members of the cast and privately invited guests."

"But did you know who all the guests were?" asked Dotty. "Look at Dad and me. We weren't invited, but Skye accepted our invitations without question and showed us to our seats. What if someone else did the same thing?"

"But surely the police would know. They took everyone's contact details," insisted Willow.

"That's true. But they might not have matched the invitations with the names. Nobody's asked Dad or me about it. And did you personally know everyone who was asked?"

Willow shuffled uncomfortably on his bench. "No, I suggested a few names, but Robbie and Skye invited most people. I was happy to leave it to them as they're locals and know who to ask."

Once again, there was silence.

Dotty sipped her tea thoughtfully, then said, "I think you should be careful, Willow. At least until the play is finished. I'll speak to Morag about extra protection and also about checking if the names on the invites matched the people who were actually there."

Jenny's phone vibrated, and she glanced at it absentmindedly. Then she grabbed it and hurriedly started tapping on the screen. She cried, "I don't believe it!"

CHAPTER TWENTY-SIX

"What's wrong?" Willow asked, his voice full of concern as he looked across at Jenny. He and Jenny were sitting opposite each other on a wooden picnic bench outside a cafe at Edinburgh Castle. Dotty and Euan were with them.

Jenny stared at her phone. "It's Toby. The police have 'taken him in for questioning'. Poor Toby, someone's filmed him being led out of the hotel by the police and he doesn't look happy."

Jenny passed her phone to Willow. "At least he's not shouting or attempting to escape. But why arrest him?"

Dotty wondered the same thing.

Jenny took her phone back and scrolled through it with her fingers.

"Here it is under 'Breaking News'. 'Actor Toby Mills has been taken in for questioning by Police Scotland after it was revealed that former MSP, Iona McDuff, had asked the police to investigate an unsolved hit and run which left one woman dead, twenty-five years ago. Ms McDuff was herself killed on stage during a play at Edinburgh's Festival Fringe in which Toby Mills is performing. It is not known at this point if the two cases are linked'."

Jenny looked up, and in a shrill voice exclaimed, "I must go to him."

"So must I," agreed Willow, starting to stand up.

Jenny sat back down. "No, Willow. I think your appearance, as Lord Thorpe, will only fuel the flames. Can you contact that solicitor who took our statements yesterday? Toby's going to need her legal expertise and no-nonsense approach towards the police. This is ridiculous. Why do the police think Toby was involved in a hit and run which happened so long ago?"

Willow carefully lowered himself back onto the wooden bench. "The police did question him that first year after our play finished. You'd had to get back to Cheltenham to start work, but Toby was being wined and dined by TV producers. One evening, a driver knocked a woman down and someone said they'd seen Toby at the wheel of the car which hit her. It was discovered he did have access to a similar car, owned by a friend, but that night he was with the scriptwriters and producers of *Driftwood Cove*. He went on to sign a TV deal with them and I didn't think any more about the case."

"But why would Iona McDuff be interested in it?" asked Jenny. "She'd only be a child when it happened."

"Perhaps she knew the woman who was killed?" suggested Dotty.

Jenny turned to her. "That would make sense. But why now? She's had plenty of time to raise it before."

"Maybe Toby's appearance at the festival brought back memories. I don't know," admitted Dotty.

Euan spoke for the first time. "Lord Thorpe, you should ring your solicitor. It's not fun being questioned without one. The police try their best to make you incriminate yourself."

"And I should go to the station and support Toby," Jenny said, standing up and climbing over the back of the picnic table bench.

"Be careful and don't get drawn into the story," warned Willow. "The press are likely to be waiting outside the police station."

Dotty watched Jenny jog down the cobbled road to the exit, weaving around tourists who were on their way to enjoy their own tour of the castle. It had become much busier since they'd sat down.

Willow was on his phone. "Good morning, this is Lord Thorpe. Please can I speak to …"

He stopped speaking and listened.

"Oh, she is. A source inside the police. Well, thank you." Willow finished his call but continued to stare at his phone. "Apparently someone at the police station tipped off our solicitor, and she was there to meet Toby when the police dragged him in."

"That's a relief," admitted Dotty. "She didn't seem to be someone the police would mess with. Hopefully, she'll deal with their questions so Toby can put the case behind him, once and for all." She looked from Willow, who was pulling at his ear, to her dad. "Is there anything else you two would like to see?"

"What about the prison? And I was going to show you round the Royal Scots Dragoon Guards Museum," said Euan.

"Well, I …" wavered Willow.

Dotty leaned forward and reassured him, "You've done your best for Toby. Let his solicitor take care of the police. And you might as well look round a bit more while you're here, rather than going back to your hotel and worrying about him."

Willow gave her a brief smile, which quickly became a grimace.

"Let's go, before it gets any busier," she suggested, as Willow continued to waver.

"The prison is fascinating," began Euan, as he also stood up. "Hundreds of prisoners were held in its dark cramped spaces, from a five-year-old drummer boy captured at the Battle of Trafalgar to Caribbean pirates."

Willow's interest was piqued, and his eyes were brighter as he said, "They sound fascinating."

Dotty followed her dad and Willow, allowing her father's extensive knowledge of the castle to wash over her as he talked to Willow.

They only looked round the top level of the prison vaults, but Dotty could imagine the dim light with prisoners sleeping side by side on wooden cots or in one of the many hammocks hanging from the ceiling.

She presumed straw would have covered the floor with rats and mice scampering about in it. She shivered and was pleased to feel the sunlight on her face as she exited the prison chambers.

The museum her dad wanted to show Willow was in the most modern part of the castle and was part of the military buildings built in the eighteenth century when the castle became a military garrison again.

"They still have an officers' mess," explained Euan, "so the General

Officer Commanding Scotland can entertain dignitaries and leading members of the military."

They entered the museum, and Dotty wandered away from her father and Willow. She was in the section dedicated to the Battle of Waterloo, looking at a model of red-coated soldiers charging forward on horses, when she heard Willow say, "So the Royal Scots Greys really did all ride grey horses."

"And this is the French Imperial Eagle which a Scottish soldier, Charles Ewart captured. And that's how the pub I often drink in on the Royal Mile, the Ensign Ewart, got its name."

"Fascinating," admitted Willow. "And so much has changed here, and in Edinburgh, since I first brought *Underground Murder* to the festival. It was an ambitious move for a relatively new, unknown theatre group, but we had great success with it."

They moved on to displays of uniforms and Dotty and Euan let Willow continue his musings.

"My wife, Suzie, was brilliant, and as director and producer she was the one who brought it all together. She wasn't much of an actor, although she did play the victim the opening year. And that was our best season. She tried to continue producing subsequent shows, but cancer and its treatment was making her weak, even back then. I had to employ a local woman, Jean, to be with Suzie.

"Jean was a great help and brought Suzie to rehearsals and shows, and helped her to feel part of it. But it wasn't the same. I continued with the festival for another five years and Jean actually took over the producer's role. She tried her best, but she wasn't Suzie, and my heart wasn't in it."

"So why bring it back this year?" asked Dotty. "Has something changed?"

They stopped to admire a portrait of Tsar Nicholas II of Russia who surprisingly, as he wasn't British, had been Colonel in Chief of the Royal Scots Greys.

"So much has changed," mused Willow, and Dotty didn't think he was referring to the fate of the Russian royal family.

"Jean is no longer with us, and I doubt Suzie will be for much longer. So this play is for them, for the two women in my life who made it possible."

"Is that Prince Albert?" asked an American woman, pushing Dotty out of the way to look at the Tsar's painting.

Euan turned to her and said, "There's no need for that. There's room for everyone."

"Sorry," apologised the woman, and in the same breath said to her friend, "No, it's someone called Nicholas."

Euan took Dotty's arm and guided her away.

Dotty saw Willow watching them and asked, "Do you have any children?"

"I, that is Suzie, couldn't have them. Not after she started treatment."

They walked on past recruitment posters. One caught Dotty's eye as it had the image of a tank parked under palm trees in front of a mosque. It was calling for soldiers to join up before the regiment left for the Middle East.

Willow was quiet, so Dotty decided to ask him more about the play. "I'm sorry your wife couldn't come up this time, but Robbie and Skye are doing a great job."

"Yes, Robbie was recommended by a friend as he helped his group out last year. He was the one that persuaded the Pleasance to allow us to use the Side Theatre. It's not a huge venue, but it is highly sought after."

"Was that the venue for your first performance?"

"The Pleasance, yes, although we were in the attic. I think it's all changed now as the Fringe has grown in size and popularity. And Skye is Jean's daughter, who helped us out back then. Robbie actually suggested her after she learnt the technical side last year, and I was delighted I could help her out. Veterinary medicine is a long degree course."

They exited the museum and walked down the stone steps onto the concourse. It was packed with people.

"Time to leave," remarked Euan. "Unless there's anything else you two want to see?"

"You've done a fabulous job, Euan, but I need to return to my flock and see what's happening. And I need to speak to the solicitor and make sure Toby is released in time for tonight's performance. We can't do it without him."

They all began to walk down the road to the castle gates. As Dotty stepped round a family consulting a guidebook, she said, "And my brain's full. But thank you, Willow, for the tickets and, Dad, for your commentary. I wouldn't have found the prison or museum half as interesting without it."

Willow bid them goodbye at the top of the Royal Mile. "See you this evening, Dotty."

CHAPTER TWENTY-SEVEN

Dotty and Euan felt weary as they returned to the flat on Broughton Street, where they enjoyed a lunch of cold meats and salads on the outdoor terrace.

"Meow." Earl Grey lifted his paw and tapped Dotty's leg. He sat beside her metal chair and was enjoying the cold meat as much as she was.

Dotty tore off a strip of chicken and dropped it onto a paving stone. Earl Grey bowed his head to eat it.

"You spoil that cat," remarked Euan.

"Probably," admitted Dotty. "But there's nobody else to. And he's accustomed to people giving him attention and titbits."

"What are you going to do this afternoon?" asked Euan.

"I thought I might sit here and enjoy the sun while I enjoy a cup of tea and read a book. Then I'll have to leave for the Pleasance and this evening's performance." No sooner had she suggested this than her phone rang. It was an Edinburgh number.

"Hello, Dotty speaking."

"Hi, it's Morag. Did you hear that Toby Mill has been brought in to answer questions on another case?"

"Yes, a cold case."

Dotty wondered if Morag had covered the phone as her voice

sounded muffled. "Hi, sorry about that. Look, can you meet me at the Pleasance in say an hour and a half? There are a few things I want to discuss with you."

"OK, and you can tell me all about Toby's arrest."

"He wasn't arrested, and I don't think he's likely to be. But again, I should know more about that by the time we meet."

After clearing away their lunch, Dotty enjoyed half an hour in the sun, starting a book she'd found on her parents' bookshelf by Edinburgh author, Ian Rankin.

Euan walked out of the flat onto the terrace and asked, "Another cup of tea?"

Dotty glanced at her watch. "No thanks. I think I'll walk to the Pleasance, so I better leave soon."

Dotty left the flat and followed a route on her phone which took her alongside the train tracks before crossing over them. The street narrowed before she walked out onto what she thought was the bottom end of the Royal Mile, but the street sign said Canongate.

There was a four-storey stone building in front of her, with wonky windows, a narrow dirty red door, and a small shop in a part of the ground floor, selling jumpers and other woollen items.

She turned right, walking uphill. This area was much quieter, although a few tourists were still wandering about. Taking the first left, she walked up the hill to the Pleasance. As usual, the Courtyard was bustling with people drinking and eating and enjoying the sunshine.

Morag intercepted her as she crossed the cobbles, heading towards the stage door.

"We can't go in just yet. It's the last performance of Agatha Christie's *A Murder is Announced* by a school drama group." Morag looked around. "And I'm starving. Do you mind if I grab something to eat? I haven't had lunch and breakfast feels a long time ago."

They wandered around the food stalls until Morag chose a haggis burrito.

Finding spaces at the end of a picnic table, they sat down. Morag bit into her burrito and then opened her mouth and waved her hand in front of it. "Wow, there's a kick of chilli in this."

"What else is in it?" Dotty asked.

"Beside haggis, there's rice, guacamole, red pepper, salad, and sour cream. It's delicious, and just what I needed. So how's your day been?"

Dotty told her about the tour of Edinburgh Castle. Then she asked, "Where's Davy today?"

"Out with his dad. And as it's such lovely weather, I suggested the beach at Portobello. I'm waiting to hear whether Gavin wants to drop him back here, take him out for his tea, or have him overnight."

"You seem pretty relaxed about it."

"Once they're together, Gavin's great with Davy. It's just getting him to commit. Sometimes I think he's worried about taking responsibility for his son, which seems ridiculous, I know."

"Not necessarily. Children aren't always easy. And he may think you're saying derogatory things about him to Davy when he's not there."

"I would never do anything like that. After all, Gavin is Davy's dad, and he needs him in his life. I just wish Gavin felt the same about Davy."

"Well the trip today sounds a good starting point."

"Och, I hope so." Morag took another bite of her burrito.

"So what news of Toby Mills?"

Morag finished chewing, wiped her mouth with a thin white paper napkin, and replied, "As I thought, he won't be charged. It was probably a waste of time bringing him in, but I think the ACC is under pressure to show some progress with the Iona McDuff case."

"But why bring up an old case?"

"What do you know about it?" asked Morag, her brow wrinkling.

"Willow told me someone thought they saw Toby driving away from a hit and run the first year they performed *Underground Murder* at the festival, but that he had an alibi for the evening."

"You do know a lot." Morag took another bite of the burrito and inclined her head, looking up into the clear blue sky.

Dotty let her finish chewing before she prompted, "So?"

"Sorry." Morag returned her attention to Dotty.

"The victim was a cleaner at one of the festival venues. She was also a friend of Iona's family, so when Iona was appointed an MSP, her mother begged her to look into the case again. Apparently, the alibi is not as tight as everyone originally thought, but Toby did meet the *Driftwood Cove* TV crew that evening."

"So the case could be closed?"

"Not exactly. Iona hired a private detective agency to speak to the TV crew but, to be honest, I think they just said what they could to get rid of the detectives. None of their stories were consistent, but it did happen a long time ago. I struggle to remember what I did last week, never mind over twenty years ago."

Morag finished the burrito and screwed up the white paper wrapping and used napkin.

"So Toby will be released?" asked Dotty.

"His solicitor will make sure of it. And although the ACC personally interviewed him, I could tell her heart wasn't in it."

"How?"

"I watched part of the interview in the room beyond the mirror."

Dotty thought back to her own police interviews and was relieved there hadn't been any fake mirrors or observation rooms attached to any of the rooms she'd been questioned in.

"And does the ACC think Toby is responsible for Iona's death, on the basis she was prying into that old case?"

"I think that's the angle she was coming from this morning, but it was clear Toby had forgotten all about the case until a private detective tried to speak to him about it. Apparently, Toby used some choice words and sent him packing."

Dotty couldn't help grinning as she thought of a private detective confronting Toby. She asked, "So what did you want to talk to me about, beside Toby?"

"Och, yes, the gun."

"Did you find any fingerprints on it?"

"It had been wiped clean, but probably quickly and in their haste the killer did leave a partial print on the barrel. I think it must be from when they hid it in the sandbag."

Dotty's pulse quickened. "Do you know whose it is?"

Morag's shoulders slumped. "No. There was no match on the database."

"So you need to fingerprint the crew?"

"I do, but if Toby is any indication, I might not have their full cooperation. He flatly refused to give his fingerprints."

"And they weren't on file from the previous case?"

Morag shook her head. "And even if they were, they'd be inadmissible as evidence as Toby requested his fingerprints be removed from the database, which they were."

"How about I collect items each of them has touched, like they do on TV?" suggested Dotty.

Morag smiled. "We don't work that way in Police Scotland. Written consent has to be given to voluntarily provide fingerprints in an investigation. Only when we have enough evidence to suspect someone, we call it probable cause, can we force a suspect to provide their fingerprints."

Dotty drew a spiral on the picnic table with her finger. "Are you saying that you have a fingerprint which would identify a murderer, but you can't force your suspects to provide their fingerprints so you can find a match?"

"That's about the gist of it."

"But what if I agree - and I know my dad will, as he wants to clear his name - to provide our fingerprints? The other crew members might follow suit. I'm certain I could persuade Willow and Jenny."

"That would be a real help," agreed Morag, "and now we should join the cast."

Dotty stood up and said, "And I'll speak to them about giving their fingerprints."

CHAPTER TWENTY-EIGHT

Dotty and Morag entered the Pleasance Side Theatre by the stage door. Immediately, they heard Toby's raised voice.

"I've better ways to spend my time than being interviewed by an Assistant Chief Constable."

"I know," Willow was trying to placate him as Morag and Dotty climbed the steps onto the stage.

Toby glanced in their direction and then strode across to confront Morag. "Why open a case from twenty-five years ago? Don't you have enough work to do with current crimes?"

"Don't blame Morag," Dotty protested. "It wasn't her idea to question you."

"So whose was it?" demanded Toby.

"Iona McDuff had been pushing us to look into the death of a family friend for months. The ACC wanted to be sure the two cases weren't connected," Morag replied.

Toby strode across to the other side of the stage, and then stopped and turned to face Willow, Morag, and Dotty. "But they're separated by twenty-five years."

Dotty stepped forward. "They are, but you were present at both of them. And in the first, a witness identified you as being the driver of the car which fled the scene …"

"But …" interrupted Toby as Jenny appeared out of the wings beside him.

"Let Dotty speak," Jenny said.

"I understand you were investigated, and you had an alibi, so no charges were pressed. But the victim was a friend of Iona McDuff's mother, and she was the one pressing for the case to be re-opened. Who wouldn't help their mum if they could?"

Willow muttered, "Totally understandable," but Jenny had to put a restraining hand on Toby, whose cheeks were still flushed.

Dotty continued, "I'm not sure if Iona asked the police to re-open the case and they refused, but she personally hired and paid for private detectives to look at it again. But can you clearly remember that evening so long ago? Those who were with you didn't give the detectives very clear accounts, and I understand you refused to speak to the one who tried to question you."

"I wasn't wasting my time dredging all that back up," confirmed Toby, crossing his arms.

Dotty said, "I don't know if Iona took the case any further, but if you were the Assistant Chief Constable, wouldn't you look into everyone who had a possible reason to harm her? And that would include a potential killer who got away with a crime but is worried they'll be convicted if the case is re-opened. You could conceivably have killed Iona McDuff to stop her investigating the cold case."

Toby squared his shoulders and took a deep breath. "Well, when you put it like that, it does sound reasonable. But for the record, I did not run some old lady over twenty-five years ago, and I did not shoot Iona McDuff on Friday evening."

Willow walked forward and said, "I hear you, and believe you. Now, do you think we can put this unpleasant incident behind us and prepare for tonight's performance?"

"That's a great idea," agreed Robbie, shepherding the students onto the stage. "We'll start by setting up the train carriage. Luckily, we won't have to dismantle it again until we're finished, as the theatre isn't being used by anyone else until Sunday. And can we test the lights after set-up, Skye?"

Skye was hanging a suit carrier on a peg above her control booth. She shouted a muffled, "Of course."

As the students set up the stage, Skye removed a pinstripe suit from the carrier and left her control booth, emerging onto the stage and handing it to Willow. "All clean, although there's still a faint mark on the sleeve where you spilt coffee on it."

Morag joined Dotty and said, "Thank you for explaining all that to Toby and for calming him down. In fact, it was very well put." She tilted her head and looked up at the theatre lights, but her phone rang, breaking into her introspection.

"Yes, Gavin." Morag listened to her estranged husband's response. "I'm glad you had fun together." Another pause. "Does he? Well I'm OK with that, but what about you? Did you have plans?"

Morag listened some more and then said, "The play starts at six thirty so if you're finished before, bring him to the main door of the Side Theatre. Otherwise, send me a message and I'll wait outside for him."

When Morag finished her call, she said to Dotty, "That's a relief. Gavin said he and Davy had a fun day together. But Davy wants to help Skye with the play so they're coming to the Pleasance and Gavin will buy Davy something to eat before the show starts."

"Davy's taken a real interest in the technical side of production," Dotty observed.

"I'm so pleased he's found something to interest him, and Skye has been a star, and very patient with him. He said she has a picture of her mum in the booth."

"I think I saw it when I had to help with the lights and sounds the first day. Willow said Skye's mum used to produce the shows, and before that she looked after his wife when she became ill, but still wanted to be in Edinburgh for the Fringe Festival."

"Such a shame she's no longer with us and can't see the final performance with her old crew and her daughter."

"Twenty minutes until curtain-up," announced Robbie.

"I better get ready," Dotty said.

"And I need to take up position by the front door. I wonder if we're expecting a full house again."

Dotty purposely avoided looking at the audience, but she had the impression the theatre had been full again on Tuesday evening.

The performance progressed without a hitch and although Dotty could tell Toby was still wound up, as he didn't stop complaining about one thing or another, he was a professional on stage and carried out his role perfectly, even adding an edge of humour at times.

Dotty caught sight of Davy several times, standing in front of Skye in the control booth, his arm outstretched as he turned off the lights or operated a switch.

After bowing for a final time at the end of the play, the cast left the stage. The students chattered loudly on a post-performance high.

Dotty was peeling off her police jacket when she heard Toby exclaim, "My agent, and he's tried calling me three times. Maybe he has a new show."

As Toby walked back onto the stage, Dotty hastily hung her jacket up on her peg below her hat and plastic bag of props. She walked down the side of the stage, keeping level with Toby but trying not to be seen.

She wasn't sure why she wanted to listen to his side of the call, but coming so soon after the day's events, she was curious to find out what role he was offered.

"What? Really? How much? Well that makes a difference, and as you said, careers have been relaunched from it. ... Yes, I know it's a risk, but what choice do I have?" Toby listened for several minutes and as he did his body tensed. "The stupid b...."

"Hi Dotty," called Davy's young, enthusiastic voice. "Did you see me today? Skye let me turn the lights on and off and press the switch with the noise of the doors opening."

Dotty smiled down at him. "That's brilliant. And I hear you had a lovely day at the beach."

Davy didn't get a chance to answer.

"I don't believe it," cried Toby.

Jenny rushed onto the stage, her hair still drawn back in a tight bun.

Dotty also stepped through the curtain wings onto the stage and Davy followed her.

"My agent just told me that the reason I was dropped from *Driftwood Cove* was because of the detectives Iona McDuff employed. The station owners heard about them and decided they didn't want to be involved with a murder investigation, so they told the producer to sack me. Talk about guilty until proven innocent."

"I'm so sorry to hear that, Toby," Jenny commiserated, removing the long hairpins which kept her bun in place, so her hair tumbled out.

Morag appeared next to Dotty and placed a hand on Davy's shoulder. "Perhaps Toby did have a motive to harm Iona McDuff after all." She wasn't as quiet as she probably meant to be, and Toby spun round.

"Do you still think I killed that irritating woman? I might have done if I'd known she'd ruined my career, but I didn't. What can I do to prove that to you people?"

Dotty stepped forward and suggested in an innocent voice, "Go down to the station tomorrow morning and voluntarily have your fingerprints taken?"

"Why on earth would I do that?" protested Toby.

The stage lights flashed on and then off again.

"Sorry," called Skye. "I knocked the switch."

Dotty explained, "Because a partial print was found on the murder weapon and if your fingerprints don't match it, then the police will leave you alone."

"Is that right?" asked Jenny, looking at Morag. "If we provide you with our fingerprints, we'll be removed as suspects."

Morag cleared her throat. "Not exactly. You could still be involved, but our current focus is to find the person who left their prints on the gun. They are our prime suspect."

"I'm going to give mine tomorrow," added Dotty, "And I'll take my dad with me. Like you, Toby, he doesn't want to be dragged down to the police station again to answer any more questions about the case."

"We should go, Toby," said Jenny.

Toby paused before replying, "OK, if it will remove me as the prime suspect. Then my agent can negotiate my deal for a place on a reality TV show I've just been offered."

"Good for you. That's great news," Jenny said.

"It certainly is," agreed Willow, joining them on stage. "And I think we should all go to the police station tomorrow and have our fingerprints taken."

CHAPTER TWENTY-NINE

After a leisurely breakfast on Thursday morning, Dotty and Euan took a taxi to St Leonard's police station.

Inside it resembled a party atmosphere rather than a sombre police station, as both Toby and Jenny were signing autographs and Willow was speaking to a young man who was holding his phone up to Willow's face.

Dotty had witnessed a journalist do this before so she could record her interview on an app on her phone.

Morag appeared and, spotting Dotty, she bustled over. "I'm pleased you persuaded the cast to turn up this morning to have their fingerprints taken, but it's like a circus in here. Anyway, come with me."

"What about Dad?" asked Dotty.

"Him too."

"Oy, Morag, what about us?" called Toby.

"Hold your horses. We'll get to everyone in time." Morag was uncharacteristically assertive, but in more of a school dinner lady manner than a police officer.

"He has a point," conceded Dotty, as she and Euan hurried to keep up with Morag. "They were here first."

"But I need to process you so we can go over the invitations from the opening night."

"Oh," said Dotty, wondering what Morag had discovered.

Morag led them down a grey-painted corridor, past a door with a Duty Nurse sign on it, into a room with various pieces of electronic equipment.

It was not dissimilar to one Dotty had been in at Cirencester Police station when her photograph, DNA and fingerprints were taken after she was arrested for a crime she was later cleared of.

"First, please read these sheets and, if you are happy, sign and print your name at the bottom and put today's date."

"What's this for?" asked Euan.

"It's confirmation you give us permission to take your fingerprints and agree that we can hold them until the case is solved and the culprit convicted, or for a maximum of two years if nobody is convicted of the crime."

"Two years is a long time," muttered Euan.

"That's only if their culprit isn't convicted," said Dotty, clearly printing and signing her name on the sheet. "And if providing our fingerprints helps the police find the culprit, it won't be so long. And you did say you'd be willing to give them if it meant the police could eliminate you from their enquiries."

"OK, OK," said Euan, signing the sheet.

The process of fingerprint taking was simple and did not involve ink and stained fingers. Instead, Morag instructed them to place the fingers, and then thumbs, of each hand on a pad as they were scanned by a machine which resembled a large office photocopier.

"I just need to check the program is satisfied with the prints you've provided," said Morag. She watched a screen and pressed buttons on a keypad. "That's the green light, and I can tell you now that your prints are not a match to those found on the gun."

"That was quick," acknowledged Euan, a note of surprise in his voice.

"So if all the cast provide their prints, you could have your prime suspect by the end of the morning," remarked Dotty.

"Let's hope so," agreed Morag, as she filed away their consent forms and switched off the machine. "I hope you don't mind being in an interview room again, Euan, but I'd like to go over the invitations and names from Friday evening while a colleague fingerprints the rest of the cast."

The small interview room Morag took them to had white walls and white plastic trunking running along one wall at waist height. The wall below it, the carpet and the chairs were the same blue used throughout the rest of the police station.

Morag left them alone for five minutes and returned with a cup of tea for Dotty and a coffee for Euan.

"Sorry to keep you waiting, but I had to brief my colleague."

Morag had also brought with her a tablet and a blue cardboard document holder. She tipped up the folder and white invitations from the opening night of *Underground Murder* spread across the table.

"I've matched some of the names on the invitations to those who were on the stage, but not all of them. Let's start with the ones you two used."

Dotty spread the invitations out and found Euan's, in the name of Simon Everett, and Scarlet Jones, which was the one she'd used. She also spotted one for Judge Arthur Marshall. Picking it up, she said, "I think this one was used by the judge's daughter, Sheena."

"The one playing the victim?" asked Morag, sounding surprised.

"Yes," replied Dotty hesitantly.

Morag tapped her tablet. "I had no idea Sheena was his daughter. He's another outspoken figure, but she seems very down to earth. Och, yes, here we are. Sheena Marshall, 19, daughter of Judge Marshall."

Morag picked up the pencil, which had rolled out of the document holder, and wrote Sheena's name above the judge's on the invitation.

"If I call out names, can you two find the corresponding invitations?" asked Morag.

Euan and Dotty worked with Morag until only three invitations remained.

Morag studied her tablet and then the invitations. "I only have two names left."

"Maybe the third is for the person who I felt brush past me in the dark," suggested Dotty.

"Could be, but unless they were the person named on the invite, we'll never find them, but let's not worry about that just now."

"Two of these invitations are for senior military officers," observed Euan. "Do you want me to ask around and try to find out who used them? They were probably junior officers."

"Do you recognise either of these names?" Morag turned the tablet towards Euan.

"No, but I can ask about them."

Morag tapped the table as she stared at the ceiling. Eventually she said, "If you're happy to do that, Euan, it might be better than if I make enquiries. People are likely to tell you the truth, whereas they'll tell me what they think I should hear."

"No, problem. Just write the names down for me."

"I'll print them off." Morag gathered up the invitations and then left with them and the tablet. She returned a few minutes later.

"The trouble," she began as she sat down again, "is that we still don't really know what happened during the blackout on Friday night."

"Why not do one of those reconstructions, like they used to do on Crimewatch?" suggested Euan.

"On what?" asked Dotty.

Morag smiled. "A TV show where police forces highlighted investigations they were struggling to solve, and they did so by filming actors recreating the crime. But how would we do it with the play?"

"The venue's not an issue," considered Dotty. "Robbie said nobody else is using the theatre until Sunday."

"And if I invite all the VIPs, I can double check the list we made, and maybe Euan won't have to make enquiries after all. I can say it's a police matter and the military must send whoever was in attendance on Friday."

Morag's eye sparkled. "And maybe we can finally work out how Iona died, and even who killed her."

CHAPTER THIRTY

Dotty slept in on Friday morning, and when she wandered into the kitchen she found a note from Karen explaining that she'd already left for the office.

Dotty reboiled the kettle and made herself a cup of tea, which she took back to bed.

Settling herself into a sitting position by propping a spare pillow behind her back, she opened the book she'd started to read the previous day.

Earl Grey stretched out and rearranged himself on top of the duvet next to her thigh. Just within stroking distance.

"What are you going to do today, boy? Another lazy day?" Earl Grey opened his mouth and yawned.

Dotty sipped her tea, being careful not to spill any on the white waffle duvet cover or her book. After about half an hour, when her cup was empty, she climbed out of bed, stretched, and padded into the bathroom.

She emerged from her bedroom twenty minutes later, dressed in a floral cotton summer dress, her hair freshly washed and dried.

The sun had reached the outdoor stone terrace, so she carried her muesli and fresh cup of tea outside, wedging her book underneath her arm as she did so.

She'd just finished her muesli when Euan appeared, carrying a cup of coffee. As he sat down, he said, "It's a real drying day. Sunny, with a slight breeze. I erected a washing line down on the communal patio."

"Umm," replied Dotty, trying to concentrate on her book.

"And it's perfect weather to throw open the French windows and air the flat."

"Right."

"We have a hoover and the cleaning things are under the sink in the kitchen."

Dotty finally placed her book face down on the table and regarded her father. "Dad, are you expecting me to clean the entire flat?"

"Well, not all of it," squirmed her father. "Anyway, you used to like cleaning and tidying up and you were very good at it."

"You used to like me cleaning and tidying up, so I had lots of practice. I'm very grateful to you and mum for having me to stay, so of course I'll help, and I'll clean my bathroom and bedroom at some point as they were spotless when I arrived."

"That was your mother."

"And today I need to do some washing. It won't be a full load, so feel free to add any things you have. It will be a dark wash."

"Oh, OK."

To placate her father, Dotty added, "And you're right, it is a lovely day to air the flat. If you hoover the living room floor, I'll clean the kitchen. How does that sound?"

"I suppose that's all right," Euan responded, although his petulant tone made it clear he didn't think it was.

"And this afternoon we're both at The Pleasance to run through what happened last Friday night."

When she'd finished her second cup of tea, Dotty suggested Euan shower and dress while she started on the chores. She was searching under the sink for cleaning products when her phone buzzed.

It was Morag telling her ACC Rhona Cameron agreed with the idea of the reconstruction and would be coming herself to supervise it.

No pressure for Morag then.

But her friend in Police Scotland still appeared enthused by the idea and sent her regular updates. The final one she received, just before lunch, told her that Morag was still trying to track down the person who'd left early but everyone else was accounted for and attending.

After another leisurely lunch on the terrace, Dotty announced, "We need to leave in ten minutes."

She and her father hailed a black taxi on Broughton Street. The driver avoided the queues on Princes Street and around the Royal Mile by taking a circuitous route to the Pleasance.

As they entered the Courtyard, they noticed a crowd gathering in the space where the red telephone box had been the previous week.

Dotty saw a man standing high above the crowd and, as she drew closer, she realised he was balancing on a small see-saw, made of a short plank of wood on a metal roller, which in turn was positioned on top of a tall stool.

The man was holding a tennis racket and as she and Euan stopped to watch, he straightened up and started bouncing tennis balls off the racket and catching them.

When one ball went astray, he managed to grab it as his legs worked madly to maintain his balance on the see-saw. The crowd clapped and cheered enthusiastically.

Dotty and Euna left the street performer and entered the Pleasance Side Theatre by the stage door.

There were lots of people inside and Dotty recognised a few faces from Friday evening.

Skye was placing props on the front two rows of seats. She consulted a piece of paper before laying a black bowler hat and an umbrella on a seat towards the far end of the second row, probably for Euan.

Willow walked onto the stage with Robbie and Morag. Morag spotted Dotty and gave her a quick thumbs up.

"Ladies and gentlemen," greeted Willow. "Thank you for sparing the time to take part in this afternoon's reconstruction of events from our opening performance. The death of MSP Iona McDuff was tragic, and I'm sure you're all as keen as I am to help the police identify and apprehend her killer."

There was a murmur of assent from the guests congregated between the front row of seats and the stage.

"Assistant Chief Constable Rhona Cameron is on her way to

oversee the reconstruction, so please sit down in the seats you were assigned on Friday, and put on any hats, wigs and glasses which you find on them. If they are different from Friday night, please let our assistant producer, Skye, know."

Skye raised her arm in acknowledgement before placing her sheet of paper in a plastic shopping bag and returning to her raised booth beside the stage. Davy was waiting for her and he whispered something and pointed at the control panel.

"Come on, Dad, let's find our seats," Dotty suggested.

The guests chattered, and there was an air of excited expectancy.

As Robbie stepped forward and started to explain how the run-through would work, Dotty noticed that there was one empty seat in her row. Was that the person who had pushed past her in the dark? Would their absence spoil the reconstruction?

The emergency exit door opened, and Dotty expected to see the authoritative face of the ACC, but instead a middle-aged man, with dark hair, wearing a t-shirt and blue blazer, walked in.

"I recognise him," whispered Euan. "Isn't he the author, Paul March?"

"That wasn't the name on the invitation," Dotty whispered back.

Robbie explained, "So we'll switch off the lights, just like we did on Friday, but then we'll switch them back on. Please don't move unless directed to do so. I'm not sure how the ACC will want to play it, but my guess is we'll go round the stage and each of you can say what you heard and felt when the lights were off and, if you moved, show us what you did."

The main door at the top of the theatre opened and everyone turned to watch Assistant Chief Constable Rhona Cameron stride down the aisle.

She reached the edge of the stage and ran her eye over the front two rows of seats. Dotty felt as if the headmistress had come to watch the school play rehearsal.

Morag walked across the stage.

The ACC asked, "Everyone here?"

"Yes, ma'am."

"Then begin."

CHAPTER THIRTY-ONE

Dotty and Euan sat at the end of the second row of theatre seats, just as they had the previous Friday before Iona McDuff was killed.

Sheena looked down the row and gave Dotty a brief wave. Dotty smiled back.

"There's an empty space in the front row," Assistant Chief Constable Rhona Cameron observed. "Should there be?"

"Ah," replied Willow, stepping out from the wings and onto the stage. He was wearing his pinstripe jacket and bowler hat and carrying a newspaper. "That was Iona's seat."

"So who's going to play her in the reconstruction?" demanded the ACC.

Willow glanced about, and his gaze fell on Skye. "Do you think young Davy can do the lights? It doesn't matter about the other sounds."

"I know how to make the noise of the doors opening and closing," said Davy in an eager voice.

"And can you switch the lights on and off when Robbie or I instruct you to?" Willow called across.

Davy nodded. A little hesitantly, Dotty thought, but then everyone in the front two rows of seats was staring at him.

"Very well," Willow decided. "Skye, you take Iona's place."

Skye squeezed Davy's shoulder before walking down the steps from the control booth and sitting in the empty seat in the middle of the front row.

"Very good," declared the ACC. "Carry on."

"At this point," explained Willow, "the theatre lights dimmed, and the 1950s music gave way to the noise of an underground train braking to a halt."

"Earls Court," announced Robbie's voice. "This is Earls Court." He stepped out of the wings on the right-hand side of the stage and there was a swooshing noise of doors opening.

"Thank you, Davy," said Willow, as he and Robbie stepped into the makeshift carriage and sat opposite each other on the left of the carriage. Willow opened his newspaper and held it in front of his face. "Doors closed please, Davy."

Dotty watched Davy hit a button, and there was the sound of swooshing again.

"Lights off, Davy."

The lights on the staged dimmed into darkness.

"Lights on."

The stage was lit up once more.

Robbie was staring at the back of Willow's newspaper as he said in his announcer's voice, "South Kensington. This is South Kensington."

Toby, wearing his flat tweed cap and jumper with holes in it, appeared on stage and, without prompting, Davy pressed the button for the noise of the train doors opening. Toby took his place, sitting with his back to Robbie.

The sound of the train doors closing was followed by the lights going off. They heard Robbie say, "Do you take this route every day, gov?"

Then the lights came back on.

Willow lowered his newspaper and nodded at Skye.

Skye stood up and looked across at the ACC who was standing erect below the control booth. She said in a nervous voice, "I came down from my booth and approached Sheena." Skye walked towards Sheena and nodded.

Sheena stood up from her seat, and just as she had on the Friday evening, she pushed past the other occupants in the row, walked up the steps to the right of the stage, and took her position in front of the imaginary doors.

Skye walked back to the empty seat in front of the middle row. "Then I asked the other guests in the second row to go onto the stage." She turned and looked at the man on the end of the row and he stood up and walked towards the stage steps. Everyone else, including Dotty and Euan, followed him.

Skye's voice was clearer, and she appeared more confident as she said, "I was waiting for the second row to file onto the stage before asking the front row to move, but Iona jumped up and climbed the stairs next to you and was the first person to stand by the left carriage door."

Skye followed the same route Iona had taken, and the other guests followed, presumably in the same order as Friday.

Skye stepped to one side so she could see the ACC and said, "I returned to my control booth and made the noise of the train slowing."

"London Victoria, this is London Victoria," announced Robbie.

Willow took up the narrative. "Then the noise of the train doors opening."

Swoosh.

"And the VIP guests filed in."

"Stop," ordered the ACC. "How did the guests know where to go?"

Robbie stood up, but Dotty doubted the ACC could see him over the heads of the guests waiting in front of the carriage door.

"I ran through with Sheena where she should sit. We attached a blood bag to her chest so in the dark, when the shot rang out, she was to press the bag and slump back against her seat, as if she was dead."

The ACC climbed the steps onto the stage and walked around the back of the makeshift carriage. She said, "And what instructions did you give Iona McDuff?"

Skye, who had stepped back into line at the front of her queue, replied, "Just the same as everyone else. To find a spare place marked with a strip of luminous yellow tape and stand or sit there. We asked the guests to react instinctively to the action, but not to speak or move."

"Very well," said the ACC. "Who was first in?"

Skye looked across at Sheena.

"I think both women entered the carriage after the noise of the doors opening," said Robbie.

"Swoosh." Davy must have heard Robbie and thought he was asking for the door to open.

Nobody moved.

"You first," the ACC indicated to Sheena, who entered the carriage and took her seat across from Toby, who just looked bored.

"So Iona had the choice of most of the carriage. Where did she go?"

"Straight for a standing position, in the middle of the carriage." Skye entered the carriage and walked deliberately across to the spot Iona McDuff had chosen.

The ACC tilted her head to one side. "Not actually in the middle. More to that side." She indicated to what was the left of the stage when seen from the front.

Dotty had thought Iona had taken the central position, but the ACC was right, she was standing behind the gap which separated Willow and Robbie.

"And nobody had told her to stand there," clarified the ACC.

Willow cleared his throat. "As Skye has already explained, only Sheena was told where to sit. The other guests were just asked to find an empty space. We thought it would look more natural."

"Very well, enter one at a time," instructed the ACC.

Euan whispered, "I wonder if she realises who the guests are. She's treating them all like children."

"Who are they?" asked Dotty from the back of the queue.

"Leading businessmen, a footballer, and an Olympic curling silver medallist, to name but a few."

"Quiet," order the ACC, and Dotty giggled as she shuffled forward in line.

The ACC questioned several of the guests about why they chose to stand in a particular position.

Then it was Euan's turn. Just as he had on the night, he hesitated and looked at Dotty.

"Go on," she urged.

"Stop," called the ACC again. "What's the matter?"

Euan gave a barely perceptible shake of his head.

Dotty gulped and replied, "My Dad hesitated on Friday evening. He wasn't happy about standing next to Ms McDuff, but the only spare places we could see were on the seats next to Willow and Robbie, and he didn't want to cause a scene, or trip over when pushing past them. I reassured him it would be OK to take the spare place next to the MSP."

"Carry on," instructed the ACC.

Euan took his place and Dotty stepped into the carriage.

"Come on, take your place." The ACC pressed her lips together as she stared at Dotty.

"This was my place. I didn't have time to find anywhere else as Robbie started speaking and, besides, there was a luminous strip on the rail."

Assistant Chief Constable Rhona Cameron walked slowly around the carriage, checking everyone's positions.

"So, Iona McDuff was standing up when the lights went out?"

"Yes," Willow agreed.

Davy must have taken her words as an instruction as the lights suddenly went out, and someone screamed.

CHAPTER THIRTY-TWO

"I'm sorry," cried Davy, and the lights flashed back onto the stage.

Assistant Chief Constable Rhona Cameron narrowed her eyes as if daring anyone in the carriage to move.

"Sorry," mumbled a young woman with curly auburn hair.

"Leave the lights on," called the ACC to Davy in a stern voice.

Davy stepped back from the control panel.

Morag, who was still standing below the booth, climbed the steps and Dotty saw her say something to Davy before she ruffled his hair. Then she turned and looked towards the stage as the ACC spoke again.

"So the lights went out. What happened next? You." she looked at Euan. "Did Ms McDuff say anything?"

Euan stuttered, "I think she cried out, but I can't remember what she said."

The ACC stared at Euan, seemingly displeased by his answer.

Dotty jumped to his rescue. "I think she called, 'I don't like this', unless that was someone else."

"Did any of you call out?" asked the ACC.

The guests all shook their heads.

The ACC turned her attention back to Euan and said, "So Ms McDuff cried out, 'I don't like this.' Anything else?"

Euan shook his head.

"I agreed with Iona," said Paul March, the author. "It was unnerving being on stage in the dark, and after the shot I panicked and left."

"You knew where to go?" asked the ACC.

"I knew where the side of the stage was, so I pushed my way out of the carriage and across to it. From there, I could see the steps illuminated by the sign above the emergency exit door. I'd had enough, so I left. Sorry." He looked across at Willow with a lopsided smile.

"OK, move towards the door as you did on Friday," instructed the ACC.

"Shouldn't we do this in order?" raised Dotty. "He said he left after the shot, but which one?"

"Which one? Ah yes, you're the only witness who said they heard more than one shot," remarked the ACC narrowing her eyes at Dotty.

"Yes, a quieter one, followed by a much louder one." Dotty stood her ground.

The ACC looked round the carriage and asked in a weary tone, "Did anyone else hear two shots?"

Three people, who were all standing close to Dotty, raised their hands.

"Of course there were two shots," said Toby in a languid tone. "I fired one of them, and whoever shot Iona McDuff must have fired the second."

ACC Rhona Cameron stared intently at him. "Unless you fired the fatal shot. You could easily have stood up, turned towards the victim, and shot her." The ACC smiled in satisfaction. "As you were supposed to be carrying a gun for the play, what a perfect way to commit the crime."

Toby jumped to his feet, his relaxed, slightly bored demeanour vanishing. "We've been through this at the station. I did not kill Iona McDuff. I had no reason to."

"That's what you say," replied the ACC icily.

"I still heard two guns fire," insisted Dotty. "If Toby fired the first one, as he says he did, then that was Sheena's cue to pretend to be dead."

"That's right," agreed Sheena. "I heard the shot, pushed the release button for blood on the fake wound on my chest, and slumped backwards. I think I also felt someone move past me."

"So we can presume that's you," Dotty looked at the author, "leaving the carriage."

"Who's in charge of this reconstruction?" the ACC demanded.

"I don't think anyone is in charge," Willow said in a conciliatory tone. "Everyone is welcome to have their say so we can piece together what happened."

The ACC crossed her arms and drew her lips together.

"Can I leave now?" asked the author. "I'm meeting my editor."

"Do you have anything else to add?"

"Only that this would make an interesting murder mystery story."

Dotty giggled and smiled at the author as he left the makeshift carriage, walked down the stage steps, and exited by the emergency door.

The ACC scowled at his retreating back, then glanced around and demanded, "So what happened next?"

Dotty looked across at Willow. "Did Ms McDuff push you out of the way and sit down in your place before or after the shot?"

The ACC's eye's widened, as if she understood the significance of the question.

"I only heard one shot," said Willow, before pausing. He appeared to be thinking. "And it was behind me, not in front as it should have been if Toby fired it."

"And where were you sitting when it was fired?" asked Dotty.

"Here," said Willow, shuffling across to the outer seat.

From the control booth Morag said, "If that was the murder shot, then you and Iona had already moved places, which supports Dotty's theory that you were the intended victim, Lord Thorpe."

"There's no such theory," blustered the ACC. "Iona McDuff was a prominent person. It's clear she was the intended victim."

Willow raised his eyebrows and in an amused tone murmured, "And I'm a nobody."

ACC Rhona Cameron had the grace to blush.

"It might be," considered Morag, "that those on the left-hand side of the carriage didn't hear the first shot because their senses were alert to movement near them as Ms McDuff and Lord Thorpe moved places."

There was a muttering of agreement from those who were standing around Skye. Skye seemed stunned by the reconstruction and stood as still as a statue, one arm clasping the nylon strap hanging from the rail, and the other hanging limply by her side.

Morag continued, "At some point it seems our victim did push Lord Thorpe out of the way so she could sit down. Unless anyone else touched him?"

Those standing near Skye, including Euan, shook their heads.

The ACC, keen to take charge again, said, "Very well, our victim pushed you, Lord Thorpe, and you moved across the seat and she sat down." She nodded at Skye, who sat down in the empty seat recently vacated by Willow.

The ACC watched and then said, "Alternatively, our killer could have shot the victim, shoved Lord Thorpe out of the way, and set the body down on the seat."

Euan cleared his throat. "But surely, I would have sensed all that, particularly if the killer dragged the body across to the seat. But I didn't."

"Neither did I," said the woman on the other side of the space where Skye had been standing.

"You might not, with all that was going on in the dark," dismissed the ACC. "What happened next?"

"The lights came back on," said Willow, "and someone shouted that Iona McDuff was dead."

"That was me," admitted the young woman with the auburn hair. "I glanced across and saw her."

"She was definitely dead when the lights came back on?" The ACC sought confirmation from the other guests.

"Oh yes," muttered several voices.

ACC Rhona Cameron strode around the outside of the makeshift carriage, stopping every few steps to consider something. When she arrived at the front of the stage, she said, "Thank you for giving up your time to be part of this reconstruction. If you remember anything else, please contact PC Elliot. Lord Thorpe, a word."

As the guests chatted amongst themselves and prepared to leave, Dotty spotted Jenny lurking in the wings at the back of the stage.

She stepped around a group of guests and joined Jenny.

"That was a waste of time. I wasn't asked about any of it." Jenny sounded disappointed.

Dotty stood beside her, surveying the stage. "It was dark, so you wouldn't see individual people, but did you notice any movement?"

"No, but I did see a gun flash."

CHAPTER THIRTY-THREE

Morag was standing beside the ACC who was still speaking to Willow. Dotty gestured to her from the back of the stage.

"I'm not sure the ACC thought that was worth her time," said Morag as she joined Dotty and Jenny.

"That's because she didn't listen," replied Jenny.

"She's convinced her theory is the correct one and she won't entertain any other ideas. But I'm beginning to think you're right, Dotty, and Willow was the intended victim. Surely the killer couldn't see who they were shooting at and aimed the gun at the seat where Willow was supposed to be sitting."

Morag looked across the stage. "I see what you mean."

"When you say you saw a gun flash, what exactly did you see?" asked Dotty.

"Gun flash?" repeated Morag.

"Yes," replied Jenny. "I was standing where I am now, watching the play. I was expecting the noise of the gun as Toby shot Sheena, but what I saw was a flash over there, on the right."

"So the left of the stage, when looking at it as the audience would," said Morag slowly.

"Willow said he heard a gun fired from behind him, so that fits what you saw," Dotty confirmed.

Morag asked, "Did you just see a flash of light, or was it more like a streak?"

"Oh, when you put it like that, I think it was a streak," replied Jenny.

"If we knew exactly what you saw, we might be able to work out where the gun was fired from?"

"Really?" asked Jenny, "but how do we replicate a gun shot in here?"

They were all silent.

"I know," cried Dotty. "We could use a torch, and flash the beam from different positions to see if anything resonates with you."

"Sure, I'm willing to give it a go," agreed Jenny. "Skye has a torch in her control booth."

"If you fetch it, Dotty," suggested Morag, "I'll tell the ACC what we're doing."

Jenny remained where she was as Dotty crossed the stage, pushing past the sandbag where the gun had been found, and climbed up the steps from the stage wings to the control booth.

She squatted down, searching for the torch, and found that it had rolled to the front. Stretching out her hand, she retrieved it, but as she did, she dislodged the piece of paper she'd found the first time she'd been in the booth.

Quickly, she returned it to its hiding place and, holding the torch, left the control booth.

Davy was standing alone on the stage, watching ACC Rhona Cameron berate his mother as she demanded, "And whose stupid idea is this?"

Jenny was right. The ACC was rigid in her view of Friday evening's events. But she'd failed to find evidence to support it, and they were no closer to establishing who the culprit was.

Morag had worked hard getting to know the crew and attending all the performances, even though she had a young son to consider. And now she was being criticised for suggesting an alternative theory. One she, Dotty, had suggested.

"It's my idea," said Dotty clearly, stepping forward. She turned to Davy and asked, "Can you go to the control booth and, when I tell you, turn off the lights?"

He nodded and scampered back to the control booth.

Ignoring the ACC's flushed face, Dotty carried the torch into the makeshift carriage. She looked across at Jenny and asked, "Ready?"

"I think so."

"Light's off, Davy," called Dotty.

In the sudden darkness, Dotty felt disorientated. She breathed deeply several times to calm herself and then held the torch up like a gun. She flashed it. Slowly, she rotated in a circle, flashing the torch until Jenny called, "Go back."

Dotty slowly turned back the way she'd come until Jenny shouted, "Stop. Do that again. But this time aim it down a bit."

Dotty pointed her torch down and flashed it once more.

"That's it. That's the flash I saw."

"Lights on, Davy," called Dotty. She blinked in the sudden glare.

From where she stood in the carriage, the torch was pointing towards the spot where Iona had been standing.

"See," declared ACC Rhona Cameron. "I was right. Iona McDuff was shot and then her body was moved. And with that cleared up, I must return to the station."

"And we have a play to perform," announced Willow.

"PC Elliot," called the ACC as she strode down the steps at the edge of the stage.

Still carrying the torch, Dotty joined Jenny at the back of the stage.

"Sorry I wasn't more help," apologised Jenny. "We're no closer to finding out who killed Iona McDuff are we?"

"No," admitted Dotty. "And this time, the culprit might get away with murder."

CHAPTER THIRTY-FOUR

Dotty wasn't sure what time it was when she woke on Saturday morning, but she hesitated before getting up.

Was it a really a week since her first tragic visit to a performance at the Fringe Festival?

"Meow," Earl Grey complained as she turned over.

Reaching out a hand, she stroked him. "What progress have the police actually made towards identifying Iona McDuff's killer?" she asked him. "And what help have I been?"

She laid her head back down on her pillow, her hand brushing Earl Grey's soft fur.

'Knock, Knock.' The taps on the door were faint.

"Come in," she called.

Karen opened the door carrying a cup of tea. As she placed it on the bedside table, Dotty pulled herself into a sitting position.

"Meow," complained Earl Grey again, before Karen picked him up and placed him on the other side of the bed. She sat down where his warm body had been curled up.

In protest, Earl Grey jumped off the bed and padded out of the open door, into the kitchen and living area.

"How are you this morning?" asked Karen. "You were rather quiet and preoccupied when you came in last night."

"It's this case. The police aren't making any progress and tonight is the last performance. After that, the cast and crew will scatter, and we may never find out who killed Iona McDuff."

"Does it mean that much to you?" queried Karen. "You didn't know the MSP, and I'm not sure you'd have agreed with her policies and what she stood for."

Dotty's hand stopped before it reached the mug of tea and she looked at her mother. "Did she believe in justice? I know she was still looking into an old case, where a friend of the family was killed, because her mother asked her to."

Karen considered the question while Dotty picked up her mug and sipped her tea.

"I suppose she did. And that people should be given a chance in life. It's just the shall-we-stay-or-leave question of independence that has dominated Scottish politics for so long. If only we could reconcile ourselves with England and move on, it would benefit everyone. I just wish we could be satisfied that we've been given our own parliament and the right to make some laws and policies. Why can't that be enough?"

"Maybe it's a question of identity, and an inherent need for some Scots to feel free to govern themselves. And it is a solid policy for any Scottish politician to rally behind."

"You're right about that. And I'm sure some of them use it as a smokescreen to hide behind rather than tackle the important issues. But that doesn't help you with your case. What's the main problem with it?"

"How it was committed. You know we did a run-through of last Friday night's play with all the VIP guests who attended?"

Karen nodded.

"During that, Jenny Church remembered she'd seen the flash of a gun firing in the dark. So we used a torch to replicate the flash. But it seems the gun was fired at Iona where she was standing next to Dad …"

"Your father wasn't the target, was he?" Her mother's voice rose. "A shot in the dark and, as the saying goes, it's an attempt at something with no certainty of success. What if someone tried to shoot Euan and hit the MSP instead?"

Dotty put her mug back on the bedside table and placed her hand on her mum's arm. "I'm sure Dad wasn't the intended victim. He only stood next to Iona McDuff because there were no other places. But you're right. From where I was standing yesterday, to replicate the gunshot, the angle had to be very specific to kill Iona."

"Where was she shot? In the back of the head?"

That was a good question and one she and Morag hadn't really discussed, but she remembered seeing the body the previous Friday evening.

"No, the side. Which does fit the location of the shooter, but for the angle of the gun to be the same as Jenny thought she saw, the killer had to be much taller, like seven feet, and nobody on the stage was that tall."

"Oh, it does seem quite a conundrum." Karen glanced at her watch.

"Sorry, Mum, I'm keeping you."

"I wouldn't be in a rush except that we have a campaign strategy meeting this morning. I'm sorry to be working on a Saturday while you're here. I'll try to be back by lunchtime."

Karen stood up to leave but stopped before she reached the door, turning back to Dotty and smiled. "I remember what I came to tell you. I've bought two tickets for your show tonight. Hopefully, I can persuade your father to join me, but if not, I'm sure Gail from the office will."

"That's nice," said Dotty, although she wasn't sure she wanted her parents at the theatre on the final evening. What if Willow was the intended victim? Tonight might be the last chance the perpetrator had to kill him.

Karen gave her a final sympathetic smile before leaving the bedroom.

Dotty sipped her tea, still thinking through the case, but not making any further progress. Sighing, she climbed out of bed and entered the bathroom.

After showering and dressing, she once again enjoyed a leisurely breakfast on the terrace at the back of the flat. It was another lovely day, although she was grateful for the pink cardigan she was wearing over her t-shirt, as the terrace was still in the shade of the surrounding buildings.

Her dad joined her, carrying a plate of toast and a cup of coffee.

"I didn't like to say anything last night, as you were clearly mulling over the afternoon's events. But I was very impressed, not only with your deductions, but the way you contested the ACC's views. Very few people stand up to Rhona Cameron."

Dotty tilted her head to one side. "Thanks, Dad." She wasn't sure she'd ever heard him say he was impressed by something she did.

"But the purpose of the reconstruction was to work out what happened last Friday evening. And that included allowing those involved to give their thoughts, and to see if the police missed anything. Jenny's recollection of the gun flash is important, even though it supports the ACC's theory and we're no closer to discovering the killer's identity."

"But you shouldn't worry. It's not your job to find the culprit," Euan reassured her.

"I know, but I'm …" How exactly did she feel? Frustrated about not working out who the killer was. Or still worried the ACC was wrong, and that Willow was the target. She said, "What if I am right? That someone wanted to kill Lord Thorpe. They might see tonight as their last opportunity and try again."

"It really isn't your concern," Euan said. He leaned back and looked up at the clear azure blue sky. "It's a lovely day. We should do something. Stop you worrying about the play and the investigation. How about an open-top bus tour?"

"I'd like that," agreed Dotty. She'd seen some of the city on foot, and the rest from inside a taxi or Morag's compact car, but she'd have a much better view from the top of a bus, and it was a lovely day to be out.

After breakfast, as she and her father prepared to leave, Dotty received a message from Morag.

No match on the fingerprints

The case had stalled and was threatening to consume her. Dotty realised she did need a break for the day, or at least the morning, and to be distracted by the sights of Edinburgh.

Dotty and Euan walked up the hill to St Andrew's Square, where men and women wearing bright red t-shirts were stopping and talking to tourists. Dotty approached a young man who asked enthusiastically, "Are you interested in an open-top bus tour?"

Dotty felt Euan tense and, concerned he might say 'no' automatically, even though this had been his suggestion, she replied, "Yes, we are. Which do you recommend?"

The man listed four tours of different parts of the city.

"We'd like the one around the old and new towns, but with commentary from a real person, rather than headphones," Dotty said.

"That's the Edinburgh Tour. The price is the same for all of them. £16 each."

"Any discount for an Edinburgh resident?" asked Euan.

"I'm afraid not," replied the man, trying to look sympathetic but eagerly producing a card reader to take Euan's payment.

Handing Euan the ticket receipts, the young man said, "Give these to your driver. Your bus has just left, so you've twenty minutes until the next one leaves. But it'll be here soon so I'd join the queue to make sure you grab yourselves seats upstairs. We're already very busy today with this lovely weather. Yours is the green and yellow bus."

Dotty and Euan crossed the road as their bus pulled to a stop beside the pavement. There was already a small queue which they joined. After showing their tickets to the driver, they climbed the stairs and found a pair of empty seats halfway down the top deck of the bus.

Euan smiled. "I haven't been on one of these for years. And what a change to see the city from up here, rather than having to fight through all the tourists."

Dotty also smiled. It was such a lovely day.

"And your mother left a message saying that she's bought us tickets for tonight's performance of your play. Despite everything that's happened with it, I never thought I'd watch my daughter perform at the Fringe. I might tell my mates to come along."

"I'm not sure about that, Dad."

"Why not? I'm proud of you. Sometimes when I look at you now, I can't believe you were once that shy, quiet schoolgirl. Even when you left to get married, you'd never have done anything like this. What changed?"

"I had to start doing things for myself after Al died. It was daunting at first but, despite a few accidents and setbacks, I've enjoyed it. Having my own income, my own cottage, and deciding what to do and when. It's fun."

"But doesn't it get lonely?" asked Euan.

"I had my friends in the Cotswolds, both at work and living next door to me, so no, I wasn't lonely. And I have Earl Grey."

"But what about a man in your life?"

Dotty looked out across the rail of the open-top bus, across to the middle of a square where a statue of a man stood on top of a tall stone column.

She replied reflectively, "There have been one or two, but whatever relationship we had ended in disappointment. Perhaps I'm better on my own."

"But what about children? You're still young enough to have them."

"I like kids," admitted Dotty. "But my own? I'm not going to rush into another relationship just for the sake of having children. If I'm going to spend my time with a man, he needs to be the right one. To treat me with respect and dignity, and not just someone who cleans the house, does his laundry, and cooks his meals."

Euan was silent as the bus pulled out and a man settled himself on a seat at the front of the bus, then announced, "Welcome ladies and gentlemen, and all you children."

The families sitting near Dotty and her dad cheered in joyous holiday spirit.

"But that's what a good wife should do. Care for her husband and attend to his needs," said Euan.

Dotty scoffed. "Like mum does?"

"No, but that's different."

"Why is it?"

"She did do all those things when you were young, and now she wants to have her own life."

"Exactly, Dad. Can't you see I also want my own life? And Mum wasn't around for me when I was young. If I have kids, I need to be content with my life so I can provide them with the best opportunities, and that's not being at home all day. It would drive me mad. I've loved learning about antiques and working at Akemans. There's more to life than sacrificing it for others."

"The Scott Monument is dedicated to the Scottish writer, Sir Walter Scott," the guide told them as the bus steadily passed a blackened stone Gothic monument, which was as tall as the buildings on the opposite side of Princes Street.

"But what man would agree to that?" asked her father.

"One who loves me and accepts me for who I am. And if I don't find him, then perhaps I wasn't meant to marry again. Or be a mother." But as she said these words, something stirred inside her.

She hadn't thought about a family of her own when she'd been married to Al. He already had a son and daughter and she'd tried her best with them. But now? Did she really want to dismiss the idea so quickly? Even so, she knew she wouldn't marry any man who came along just to father her child.

"As long as you're happy," smiled her father as he laid a hand on her thigh. "That's the important thing."

Dotty stared up at Edinburgh Castle, rising above them and wondered. Was she happy?

CHAPTER THIRTY-FIVE

Dotty was more nervous about the final performance of *Underground Murder* than she had been for any of the previous shows.

Her fingers trembled as she fastened the buttons of her police jacket.

Was it just that this was the last show? There was certainly an atmosphere amongst the crew. But was it excitement or trepidation?

"Don't do that!" Toby shouted at someone she couldn't see.

Even Willow, normally so level-headed, had snapped at a journalist when asked if a member of his cast was a murderer.

Dotty was fastening the brown wool coat she wore over her police jacket for the first act when Euan appeared.

"I've been thinking over what you told me this morning. About the killer trying again," he said hesitantly. "And there is something you could do, just in case they make another attempt on Lord Thorpe's life." He handed her a small telescope-like object.

"This is a night-vision scope. It should fit in your pocket." He eyed her coat.

"You know by now when the stage lights are turned off, so just before they are, close your eyes. Open them again when it's dark and remove the scope. You can use it to check nobody is moving around in the dark or acting suspiciously."

"Thanks, Dad," said Dotty as she hugged him. "This makes me feel much better. I can actually do something. And if the play goes without a hitch, all the better."

"I should return to your mother."

"And Dad," said Dotty as Euan started to turn away, "thanks for coming."

"Five minutes," called Robbie as Euan left.

"Ready," said Jenny, as she joined Dotty. "Remember to relax."

"I'm not sure I can tonight," Dotty replied.

"I know what you mean," admitted Jenny. "Everyone's so tense. But hopefully once the play starts, we'll get into a rhythm. After all, this is our last ever performance." She gave Dotty a nervous smile and returned to the back of the stage.

Dotty saw Morag and Davy standing in the wings, near the sandbag. Without stepping out onto the stage, she crept along the backstage area to reach them.

"Everything OK?" asked Dotty.

"Davy wants to join Skye for the last time, but I'm nervous. There's a funny atmosphere amongst the crew."

"It's just last night nerves," Dotty reassured her. "And I'm sure being up in the control booth with Skye is as safe a place as any."

"Please, Mum," begged Davy.

"Och, off you go. But don't annoy Skye. She seems the most nervous of the lot."

Which was unexpected, thought Dotty.

Davy climbed the three steps from the side of the stage to the raised control booth.

"The ACC and the Chief Constable are here. And I saw your parents," Morag said.

"Mum bought tickets and, surprisingly, Dad agreed to come with her."

Sheena climbed the stage steps and as she passed them confided, "And my father, the judge, has come. I can't believe how nervous I am."

"You'll be fine," Dotty called to her retreating back.

Morag craned her head and stared out into the theatre. "Full house I'd say."

"Where are you going to sit?"

"I've a reserved seat at the end of the fifth row back. So if there is any trouble, I can be on hand quickly."

"Let's hope there isn't." Dotty crossed her fingers.

A whisper spread around the backstage area. "Everyone take your places."

"Oh, I nearly forgot," said Morag. "I thought you might like to see the summary of the gun report, although we still haven't identified the fingerprints." She passed Dotty a brown envelope and just before she descended the stage steps, she added, "Break a leg."

Dotty smiled feebly after her.

Dotty took her position for the start of Act 1, stuffing the envelope into her coat pocket along with the night vision scope.

Willow strode out onto the stage, wearing his pinstripe suit and bowler hat, and held up his arms.

In a voice Dotty could imagine him using in the House of Lords, he announced, "Thank you for attending our final performance of *Underground Murder*. It's been quite a journey, from the opening of the play here at the Pleasance twenty-five years ago, to tonight's performance. During that time there have been successes, such as Toby Mills' sterling television career and Jenny Church's rise to a world-class stand-up comedian. But there have also been tragedies. My dear wife Suzie, the first director of the show, cannot be with us because of her terminal illness, and her successor, Jean, mother of our assistant producer Skye, sadly passed away last year."

Willow looked across at Skye and Dotty was disturbed by the malicious look on Skye's face. Even Davy stepped to one side, as if feeling her hostility.

But if Willow had noticed Skye's expression, he chose to ignore it and continued, "So I hope you enjoy the last ever showing by The Spa Players of *Underground Murder*."

The audience clapped loudly, and Jenny whispered, "Here we go." The lights on stage dimmed as the sound of an underground train filled the theatre. Willow and Robbie, complete with his Elvis-style wig and black leather jacket, stepped onto the stage.

Dotty patted her pocket again. She glanced at the makeshift carriage. Did she have time to read the summary report Morag had given her?

Turning away from the stage, she opened the envelope and removed a folded sheet as the lights switched off. When they came back on, she unfolded the paper and, as her eyes became accustomed to the light, she skimmed the gun report. Specific words jumped out at her, including 'Swiss design', 'two shots' and 'used by veterinarians'.

The lights went off again.

She stuffed the paper and envelope back into her pocket and stepped onto the stage, taking up her position behind Sheena.

As she had for the previous four nights, she sat down opposite Sheena in the makeshift carriage, next to Toby, surrounded by all the actors and students. Only Jenny wasn't with them, and Dotty knew she'd be watching from the back of the stage.

Just before the lights went out, she shut her eyes and reached into her pocket, clasping the night vision scope.

Feeling the surrounding darkness, she removed the scope and held it up to her eye. Nobody around her, in the right-hand section of the makeshift carriage was moving. She twisted round and scanned the rest of the stage. And froze.

Skye was creeping across the stage, and she was carrying a gun. A gun used by veterinarians, the report had said.

Skye appeared to be counting, and when she reached a point behind the seat where Willow was sitting, she raised the gun.

"Davy, lights," shouted Dotty.

The lights flashed on and some of the crew gasped.

Dotty jumped up from her seat and stood, facing Skye.

Skye was motionless, like one of the festival's human statues, her arm raised, a gun pointing at Willow's head.

Robbie threw himself forward and dragged Willow to the stage floor as a shot rang out. And then another. Dotty didn't think the gun could fire a third, but it didn't matter. Two of the students had rugby tackled Skye to the floor.

Some of the audience started clapping and others joined in. "They think it's part of the play," whispered Sheena, who had also stood up and joined Dotty. "I can see my dad looking really confused as I told him I was the victim."

"Think yourself lucky, tonight you're not," muttered Toby, his voice shaking. He remained in his seat but had turned to watch the action. "Those shots were lethal. It was quick thinking by Robbie to pull Willow to the floor and use the seats between them and Skye as a shield. I don't think either of them are hurt."

Morag was running up the stage steps and, behind her, the ACC was striding down the aisle.

A whisper started somewhere in the theatre, and Dotty could hear it spread through the audience. A woman cried out and there were gasps as people realised that the drama they'd seen on stage wasn't part of the script.

Dotty remembered the hidden piece of paper in Skye's control booth. She crossed the stage, knocking into the sandbag where Skye had hidden the first gun after mistakenly shooting Iona McDuff. Climbing the three steps into the booth, she was greeted by a white-faced Davy.

"Was that supposed to happen? Why did Skye go onto the stage with a gun?"

"I'm not sure," replied Dotty, although she thought she might know why Skye wanted Willow dead. "But well done. You did a fantastic job turning the lights on."

"I did?" Davy looked at her and she smiled in reassurance.

He smiled back. "Are we finishing the play?"

"I'm not sure. But before we do, there's something I need. Can you reach down under the control panel and find a sheet of paper that's wedged there?"

Davy did as requested and after fumbling about, he reappeared, holding up the sheet of paper. "Is this it?"

"Yes, thank you. And we better give Skye the photo of her and her mum."

Davy pulled the photo out from where it was wedged at the end of a panel.

As he gave it to Dotty, he said in rather a grown-up voice, "I'm not sure Skye will feel like operating the controls tonight. She looks very upset. I'll stay here and you, Willow or Robbie, can tell me when to turn the lights off again."

"OK, Davy, you do that."

CHAPTER THIRTY-SIX

Dotty hovered behind Morag, who clasped Skye's arm.

"What is going on?" demanded the ACC, her face flushed.

"Dotty was right. Willow, Lord Thorpe, was the intended victim," replied Morag.

Willow was dusting himself down. He looked across at Skye with an expression of pure love. As he staggered across to her, Dotty noticed the tears glinting on his cheeks. He threw his arms around Skye and hugged her. Dotty heard him mutter, "You poor, poor girl. It's all my fault."

"Can someone please explain what is going on?" demanded the ACC for a second time.

"Perhaps," suggested Dotty, "Morag should accompany Skye to the station. You may want to go with them, before the press descends on the theatre. I'm sure the events on stage are already flying around social media. But in an attempt to hold back the tide, perhaps we should continue with the play and allow everyone some breathing space."

"But the stage is a crime scene," responded the ACC.

"And we caught the culprit red-handed. I don't think Skye will deny what she did, and you have at least eighty witnesses who saw her fire the gun. But if you want their statements, you'll need more manpower, so finishing the play will give you time to organise it. And you might want this."

Dotty handed Morag the paper which had been wedged under the control panel. She also pushed the photograph into Skye's hand and felt the younger woman's fingers tighten around it.

Willow cleared his throat. "I think we should finally listen to Dotty, and in tribute to everyone involved, finish the play."

Robbie joined them, and as he handed a spent bullet to Morag, he asked, "But what about the technical side?"

"I think Davy can manage it, with a few prompts from us," reassured Dotty.

Dotty, Willow, Robbie, and Morag all turned to look at Davy who waved back at them.

Willow called, "Are you ready to restart?"

Davy gave him the thumbs up.

As Morag led Skye out of the theatre by the emergency exit door, Dotty finally became aware of the chatter from the audience.

Willow stepped to the front of the stage. "Ladies and gentlemen. I apologise for the delay, but we are now ready to restart the play." His manner was dignified as he returned to his seat in the makeshift carriage and picked up his newspaper.

Dotty rushed across to her seat and called, "Davy, lights!"

The lights turned off, and a hush descended on the theatre. There was the sound of a shot and with the noise of train brakes, the lights turned back on. Sheena was leaning back in her seat, a red stain across her chest.

Dotty did relax as the play progressed, despite forgetting her handcuffs again. The audience laughed when Robbie's hand extended out of the wings holding them, and she bowed in acknowledgement of her mistake.

"I'm glad that's over," remarked Jenny as they left the stage together at the end of the final scene.

The clapping began and Dotty, Sheena, and the students stepped onto the back of the stage and bowed.

As the clapping increased, the actors took their applause until Willow once again stepped forward, holding his hands out in front of him as he asked the audience to be quiet.

"Once again, thank you all for coming, and I hope you enjoyed our performance. And please show your appreciation to our stand-in technical assistant, Davy."

Willow turned to the raised control booth and lifted his hands as he began to clap. The rest of the cast followed his lead and, after a moment's hesitation, so did the audience.

Davy beamed at Willow and the cast on stage. He then turned to the audience and, perhaps realising for the first time how many people were watching him, he turned bright red and ran down the steps and into the wings at the side of the stage.

The ACC climbed the steps beside the emergency exit and held her hands up for quiet. "Ladies and Gentlemen. A serious crime was attempted this evening. Luckily, no harm was done, but my officers will need to interview each of you before you leave. I apologise for the inconvenience."

Dotty followed the rest of the cast off the stage and was unbuttoning her police jacket when Davy appeared. His face was white, and he looked scared. "Where's my mum?"

"She had to go to the police station. Would you like to stay with me?"

"Yes, please." Davy pressed his lips together and nodded. He looked about to cry, which wasn't a surprise. It had been an eventful evening.

"Why did Skye want to hurt Willow? She's my friend. But so is Willow. I don't understand," said Davy in a small voice.

Dotty squatted down so she could look him in the eye. "I'm not sure I do, but sometimes adults hurt each other. And some believe other people have hurt them."

"You mean like my dad leaving Mum and me? Mum doesn't know, but sometimes I hear her crying. Is it my fault Dad left?"

"No, of course it's not," Dotty reassured him. "But sometimes adults need space away from each other to think."

"Is that what my dad's doing? Is he thinking? When will he finish? Will he come home?"

"If you and your mam will let me," said a man with a strong Scottish accent.

"Dad!" cried Davy, flinging his arms around the man's waist.

To Dotty he said, "Hi, I'm Gavin. Morag called and asked me to collect Davy. She said she'll be working all night."

"I'm Dotty. And poor Morag,"

"Och, at least she caught the culprit."

"No, Dad. That was Dotty," said Davy in a serious tone.

"But I couldn't have done it without you, Davy. You saved Willow's life."

Davy's cheeks flushed. "Did I really?"

"Yes, you did. And you were a fantastic technical assistant."

Davy turned to his dad and asked, "Would you like to see my control booth?" Davy grabbed his father's hand and pulled.

Gavin smiled at Dotty, before allowing his son to lead him down the backstage area to the raised control booth.

Dotty hung up her jacket but wondered who would collect it since Skye was no longer with them.

Jenny appeared with a large red canvas bag. "Throw your props in here. Willow asked me to collect everything but keep them together in case the police want to look at them."

"Pop!"

Dotty jumped.

Jenny laid a hand on her shoulder. "It's only champagne, well Prosecco. Willow ordered it for the audience since they're hanging around waiting to be interviewed by the police. Go grab a glass. You probably need one after what happened."

"I'm not sure I feel like drinking," replied Dotty as she picked up the plastic shopping bag of props, her wig and her police jacket, and placed them into the red canvas bag.

"Well, I definitely need a drink after that performance," announced Karen as she joined them. "And I grabbed a glass for you, but if you don't want it?"

"I'll have it," said Jenny, taking the spare glass from Karen.

"This is just a short break for you, isn't it?" Karen asked her. "When does your one-man show start?"

"Tuesday," Jenny replied.

"I've got tickets to watch it on Thursday," Karen said. "What about you, Dotty?"

"I haven't had time to organise any," muttered Dotty.

"Then you must join Willow and Toby on Tuesday. And bring Morag with you. Robbie said he can't make it and I don't think Skye will be using her ticket."

There was a short silence, which Jenny eventually broke. "I better finish collecting props." Still holding the glass in one hand, she dragged the red bag across to some students.

"Where's Dad?" Dotty asked.

"With the police. Did he really give you a night vision scope?" asked Karen.

"I think he was worried about what might happen in the dark. And perhaps he believed my theory that Willow had been the intended victim all along."

"Willow?"

"Lord Thorpe."

"But why?"

"Because Skye blamed him for her mother's death."

CHAPTER THIRTY-SEVEN

Dotty and her mum watched police officers as they searched the stage, presumably for the second bullet. Morag had taken the gun with her when she'd led Skye away.

An officer poked a pen into the back of the makeshift carriage seat where Willow had been sitting, and dragged out a metallic object, which he dropped into a transparent evidence bag.

Assistant Chief Constable Rhona Cameron joined him, and he handed her the bag, which she held up to the light. The officer slipped away, leaving the ACC alone.

She turned and, spotting Dotty, strode across the stage and declared, "You shouldn't have interfered."

"I didn't," Dotty contested. "All I did was watch what was happening on stage through a night-vision scope. Anyone could have done it."

"But still …"

Karen stepped towards the ACC and, holding her head high, remarked, "How about 'congratulations' or 'thank you' for what my daughter did."

"Your daughter," spat the ACC, "acted recklessly."

"My daughter saved a man's life. The problem you have is that she showed how incompetent the police have been. And you," she raised her finger to the ACC's face, "refused to listen to anyone else's opinion. I hope you've learned that it's better to consider other people's theories and views of cases, even if they differ from your own. That way, you may improve your clear-up rates. Come on, we're going."

Karen grabbed Dotty's arm, but the ACC cleared her throat.

"I am grateful for your vigilance, and your quick action. Perhaps I should have listened to you, but I still don't really understand what happened," admitted the ACC. "So I'm going to need you to accompany me to the station for an interview and debriefing."

"Tonight?" exclaimed Karen.

"It's OK, Mum. I'll have to go through it some time, and probably better tonight while it's fresh in my mind. Besides, I feel I should keep Morag company."

"Constable Elliot is a police officer," declared the ACC.

"But she's also a mum with a young son, and she's been trying to organise his care around working long hours, and late into the evening this past week."

The ACC wrinkled her nose before admitting, "I'm also a mum."

"And where are your children?" asked Dotty.

"On holiday with their grandparents."

Dotty broke the silence which followed by asking, "When shall we leave?"

The ACC glanced around. The theatre was less crowded than it had been, and she said, "My officers seem to have everything under control here. Now is as good a time as any."

"How will you get back? Shall I wait up?" asked Karen.

"I'll make sure a police car brings her home," replied the ACC. "But I've no idea what time we'll finish."

Dotty smiled at her mum. "I'll be fine. Don't worry."

"If you're sure? I won't wake you in the morning. I'll let you have a lie-in."

"Thanks, Mum," Dotty replied as she and the ACC left the theatre.

At St Leonard's Police Station, a police constable escorted her to an interview room. "I was told to offer you food and a drink. I don't recommend our ready meals, but we have some sandwiches left over from earlier if you'd like some of those."

Dotty's tummy rumbled, and she glanced at her watch. It was a quarter past ten. "Sandwiches and a cup of tea would be lovely."

The constable left and, looking around the blue-furnished room, Dotty wondered how long she'd have to wait to be interviewed. The constable soon returned with a strong cup of tea and a plate of assorted sandwiches and, balanced on top of them, a chocolate bar.

Alone, she munched her sandwiches, feeling both relief at having saved Willow's life and finally working out who'd killed Iona McDuff, and anguish for not having solved the puzzle sooner.

But even if she had, she couldn't have prevented Skye from being arrested, as she'd already killed someone. How tragic it all was.

She'd just finished her bar of chocolate when the door opened and the ACC strode in, followed by Morag.

Morag grinned at her as the ACC said, "Good, you've been looked after." She turned to Morag and asked, "Can you fetch some glasses and some still and sparkling water? The good stuff."

Morag left them as the ACC sat down opposite Dotty. She didn't say anything, so neither did Dotty until, several minutes later, Morag returned carrying three plastic glasses and two glass bottles.

As Morag settled herself, the ACC pressed a button on the recording equipment on the table and said, "Present: Assistant Chief Constable Rhona Cameron."

Morag added, "Constable Morag Elliot."

She looked at Dotty, who cleared her throat, and said, "Dorothy Sayers."

The ACC said, "Please run through this evening's events."

Dotty began. "Before the play started, my father gave me a night vision scope and instructions on how to use it. This morning I'd told him about my concerns regarding the play, and that if someone wanted to kill Willow, Lord Thorpe, tonight might be their last opportunity. He told me that when the stage was in darkness, I could use the scope to reassure myself nothing untoward was happening."

"But it was," said the ACC.

"Yes, and to be honest, by then I was expecting it."

"Why?"

"Because I'd skimmed the summary gun report Morag, PC Elliot, handed to me just before the play began. It said the gun was a specialist one, used by veterinarians for humane killing. Skye is studying veterinary science at university and it's conceivable she had access to such a weapon. And I didn't think she'd given her fingerprints to be eliminated from those on the gun."

"But you didn't know that for sure," replied Morag. "Besides, Robbie Campbell hasn't provided his fingerprints either."

The ACC glanced at Morag and then back at Dotty. "So what did you see through the night scope?"

"Skye on the stage, carrying a gun and moving stealthily towards the chair where Willow was sitting. Her face was screwed up in concentration and she appeared to be counting."

"Counting?" queried the ACC, drawing her eyebrows together.

Dotty turned to Morag and asked, "Do you have that sheet of paper I gave you?"

"Och, aye. I'd forgotten about it." Morag removed the folded paper from her pocket and placed it on the table. It was the plan of the stage which had been hidden in the control booth.

Dotty opened it up and glanced down at the bottom left of the sheet. It was as she remembered, two sets of numbers. Turning the paper back to face the ACC and Morag, she pointed to the numbers with her finger.

"I think these are steps which Skye had calculated, so she knew how many to take in the dark to be in the right position to shoot Willow. She'd have had plenty of time during rehearsals and preparing for the play to work out where to stand, the angle to hold the gun and the direction to walk when she left the control booth and navigated the steps onto the stage."

"There are two figures," noted Morag.

"I think the second is to the sandbag, which she'd probably opened up before the play started so she could hide the gun in it. I remember now, on that first night, that after the sound of the two shots being fired, there was a delay. Someone, probably Toby, muttered about the lights.

"I think we had to wait for Skye to hide the gun and return to her control booth to press the button for the noise of the train brakes. We heard those and the announcement of the station before the lights came back on. All of this would have given Skye time to sort herself out so that it appeared as if she'd never left her control booth."

"It must have been a shock to her when she discovered it wasn't Willow's dead body in the seat, but Iona McDuff's," Morag said.

"I expect so, and she daren't try again, with everyone alert to what might happen, until tonight."

The ACC leaned forward. "Because, as you said earlier, this was her last opportunity."

Dotty nodded as the ACC unscrewed the cap of one of the bottles. "Sparkling water?" she asked.

Dotty picked up a glass and waited for the ACC to pour the fizzing liquid into it.

As the ACC poured a glass for herself, she considered, "But why? What reason does Skye Richie, a veterinary student at Edinburgh University, have to kill a peer of the realm?"

"Abandonment, loss, and she may well have blamed him for her mother's death," replied Dotty.

"But according to our investigation, her mother died of cancer," countered the ACC.

"But she died alone, with only Skye for comfort. Which is probably why Skye blamed her father."

"Her father?" queried the ACC.

Dotty fiddled with her glass. "I believe Lord Thorpe had an affair with Skye's mother. He was probably seeking solace himself, since his wife was terminally ill, although ironically, she's outlived Skye's mother. And Skye's mum helped look after Lord Thorpe's wife, and then produced the play when Suzie no longer could. I suspect that in those early years, Willow doted on his young daughter when he was in Edinburgh."

"But then the theatre group stopped performing at the Fringe Festival, and he never recognised her publicly. Never acknowledged Skye as his daughter," mused Morag.

"He probably felt he was protecting his wife and intended to claim Skye as his own after she died," suggested Dotty.

"But Lord Thorpe's wife is alive. Skye's mother is dead. And Skye is hurt, angry, and focuses her blame on the man she believes is her father. We will, of course, need to hear Lord Thorpe's side of the story and, if he is willing to provide DNA, confirm he is Skye's biological father," said the ACC.

"Skye believes Willow abandoned her and her mother, as you said." Dotty looked at the ACC. "But if you look into the trust fund that paid her school fees, and is now supporting her through university, I wouldn't be surprised if Lord Thorpe is the benefactor."

"A hidden backer. If only Lord Thorpe had been more open, if you are right about the trust fund, or had reconnected with Skye's mother, he may have averted this tragic event, and a long prison sentence for his daughter."

The three of them were silent.

"Ma'am, do we need to keep Mrs Sayers any longer, or do you think she can go home now?"

The ACC sipped her water. "I don't think there's anything else you can add tonight, although we may need you to answer further questions. And now we must see if Skye Richie's lawyer has arrived and start interviewing her. It's going to be a long night."

CHAPTER THIRTY-EIGHT

Dotty woke up late on Sunday morning although she didn't feel completely refreshed.

"It's so sad what some people do to each other," she said to Earl Grey who was curled up beside her. "If only they'd speak to each other, really talk, not just the pleasantries, and listen. But none of us is perfect."

She climbed out of bed, found her slippers, and pulled on the white waffle dressing gown. Still rubbing her eyes, she wandered into the kitchen.

A lean pair of arms immediately encircled her, and she smelt a floral scent. Finally, her mum let go and walked across to the kettle, switching it on. "I'm afraid we can't sit outside today. After the lovely weather we've had, it's back to rain."

With fresh cups of tea, they both sat down at the small circular kitchen table.

"How did everything go last night, at the police station?" Karen asked.

"It was fine. Just an interview with Morag and the ACC to run through the evening's events. They hadn't actually spoken to Skye, she was waiting for a lawyer."

"Any idea why she wanted to kill Lord Thorpe? And what about Iona McDuff?"

Dotty ran through her own theories of the shooting and attempted shooting.

"I've very proud of you, and so is your dad. You should have heard him on the phone to his mates last night, bragging that you'd solved the Iona McDuff case for the police. And of course, playing up his role in it. He'll dine out on the story for the rest of the year."

Dotty smiled. "I didn't do it for the fame, or to get one over on the police. It was just a problem which needed solving. Justice that needed serving. Even though the guilty party turned out to be a young woman who felt so wounded that her view of her life, and the people in it, was skewed."

"Is this what you're going to do now? Be a private investigator?"

Dotty laughed as the image of herself wearing a Sherlock Holmes deerstalker hat popped into her head. "No thanks. I'll stick with antiques."

On Tuesday evening, Dotty finally had a chance to catch up with Morag at the Pleasance Courtyard before they both attended the opening night of Jenny Church's stand-up comedy show.

"You look shattered," Dotty said.

Morag smiled thinly. "I only caught a couple of hours' sleep at the station on Friday night, and I've worked all weekend tidying up loose ends in the Skye Richie case. There was a stabbing on the Royal Mile on Saturday night, so most of the officers have been transferred to that investigation."

"Has Skye been charged?"

"Yes, with the murder of Iona McDuff and, despite his protests, the attempted murder of Lord Thorpe. Did you know he organised the lawyer for her?"

"No, but I'm not surprised he did. I saw the look of pure love on his face after Skye tried to shoot him."

"Well, the solicitor was the same officious woman who acted for him, Jenny, and Toby Mills, earlier in the week. She's claiming mental disorder, and that Skye was 'unable to appreciate the wrongfulness of her conduct'."

"It's a good try," replied Dotty, "But I don't see how she can argue that without proving Skye has a mental illness, but that's one for the doctors and lawyers to sort out."

"I agree, and for someone else in my team to deal with. Me, Davy and Gavin are going away to Poolewe on the west coast. There's a wonderful empty beach for Davy to play on, and I'm going to relax and perhaps wander around Inverewe sub-tropical gardens. Gavin has rented a cottage cheaply from a workmate."

"I'm so pleased for you. You'll have a chance to spend time together as a family."

"Yes, and I think Gavin has realised that's what we are, a family, but we each need our space and our work. He says we need to learn to be, how did he put it, interdependent."

"That sounds positive."

Morag raised her glass of Diet Coke. "I'll drink to that." Then she asked, "Has the ACC been in touch?"

"With me? No, why should she?"

"I think she wants to nominate you for a Chief Constable's Bravery and Excellence Award, although the winners won't be announced until next year."

Dotty smiled. "It's more praise than I ever received from the Gloucestershire Police. They preferred to award me with a night in the cells."

Morag narrowed her eyes in confusion and for the next ten minutes Dotty told her about her experiences helping the police in Cirencester.

"Good evening," announced Willow, standing beside Morag and Dotty's picnic table.

Toby Mills hung back, speaking to someone on his phone.

"First things first. How is my daughter?" asked Willow.

"You know her fingerprints match those found on the gun?" Morag said.

"I had heard."

"And the spare key to the room where the humane guns and poisons were kept at the university's veterinary department was found in her mum's house, where she's been living by herself for the past year. I don't think anything has changed. Skye still sleeps in the smaller room and her mother's clothes were in the wardrobe of the larger bedroom, and her toiletries in the bedroom and bathroom."

"Poor girl," sighed Willow. "She hasn't been able to grieve. Has she seen the psychiatrist I organised?"

"I believe he's visiting her tomorrow morning."

"Good, and I'll go in the afternoon, even though she still refuses to speak to me."

Toby finished his call and approached them, grinning. "My agent has negotiated an increase in my fee for the reality TV show to £300,000. And I'm staying up here as filming starts in September, in a Scottish Castle."

"What's the show about?" asked Dotty.

"I'm not entirely sure, but it sounds fun. It's called Betrayers."

Dotty thought it sounded right up Toby's street.

"And," Willow declared, "we have to make sure we're lively and laugh at all Jenny's jokes tonight. A US talent scout is watching and considering her for her own show in Las Vegas."

"Wow!" Morag exclaimed. "That would be amazing."

"And what about you two?" Willow asked, looking down at Dotty and Morag.

"I'm going on a family holiday to the west coast," Morag replied.

"I'm not sure," Dotty said. "I'll spend a couple more weeks with my parents in Edinburgh before deciding what to do next."

"Do you have a job to go back to?" asked Willow.

"Yes," Dotty replied hesitantly, "but I'm not sure if it's the right one at the moment. Don't get me wrong, I love the antiques world, and my colleagues at the auction house and my friends in the Cotswolds, it's just that …" her voice trailed off.

"You need some adventure," suggested Toby.

"Oh, I'm not sure I want anything too exciting … or dangerous. But, yes, I need to experience more of life. I'm just not sure how, where, or doing what."

"Oh, to be young with no ties. There are so many places you could travel to," said Willow in a dreamy tone.

"I do have my cat," protested Dotty.

"Why would that stop you?" asked Willow.

"I suppose it shouldn't," Dotty replied as a figure wearing a kilt started playing the bagpipes.

Willow leaned closer to Dotty and asked, "Have you seen the Tattoo?"

She shook her head. "My dad couldn't get us tickets, even with his military contacts."

"Give me a minute." Willow walked away, leaving Dotty, Morag and Toby listening to the bagpipes.

The crowd applauded, and the piper moved on.

"How very atmospheric," Morag declared.

Willow returned and asked, "Are you and your father free on Thursday night?"

"I think so," Dotty replied hesitantly.

"Good, because I've found you two tickets for the Tattoo."

Dotty smiled broadly. "That's brilliant. Dad will be delighted."

"But you'll have to dress up. We're all guests of Lord Arbermarle, in his private box."

"Och, private box, and two lords. You're moving up in the world," joked Morag.

Willow glanced at his watch. "And now we need to find our seats for Jenny's show."

CHAPTER THIRTY-NINE

On Thursday night, Dotty stood in front of a full-length mirror in her bedroom at her parent's flat.

"Perfect" Karen complemented her. "Not too fussy but still smart and very elegant."

Karen had dismissed Dotty's summer dresses for attending Edinburgh's Military Tattoo as a guest of Lord Arbermarle.

Instead, she'd persuaded her to try on some of her own outfits. Dotty finally chose a simple tartan shift-style dress with a matching wool jacket, angled across her chest and fastened with large bone buttons.

As she considered her reflection, she smiled. She felt smart enough to mix with Willow and his titled friends, without worrying about tripping over a long evening dress.

"And to finish it off." Karen bent down and pinned her regimental brooch on Dotty's jacket.

"But I can't wear that," protested Dotty.

"It's for wives and daughters of men in the regiment, so you have every right. And it'll make your father proud if you wear it tonight."

Dotty slipped into a pair of plain navy ballet-style shoes with only a small heel. She didn't want to be tottering around this evening and her dad had told her they might have quite a walk, even though they were in one of the private boxes.

As Dotty and her mum left her bedroom, Euan prised the cork out of a bottle of champagne.

"I was given this when I left the regiment, and I've waited for a special occasion to open it. I think accompanying my daughter to the Tattoo as guests of Lord Thorpe and Lord Arbemarle is the right one. And don't you look stunning?"

Her dad smiled proudly as he handed her a glass of champagne. He was wearing a black evening jacket and bow tie with tartan trousers, and a row of medals on his chest.

Karen held up her glass and toasted, "To us, together again as a family."

"To us," chorused Euan and Dotty.

Euan had been right. The Tattoo was really busy, with a queue of people snaking their way from the castle gates, down part of the Royal Mile and then on into a side street.

Following the instructions Willow had provided with their tickets, and the large, embossed invitations he'd had delivered to the flat, they approached a steward standing by the entrance gate.

After examining both their tickets, he ushered them through. "Box 4, on the left."

They climbed a flight of metal stairs and entered Box 4, which was open at the front, looking out over the esplanade and Edinburgh Castle.

"Dotty, wonderful to see you," Willow greeted them. "Let me introduce you to our host, Lord Arbermarle. But first, a drink."

After her earlier glass of champagne, Dotty chose sparkling water and Euan asked for a beer.

"Tony, these are my friends, Dotty Sayers, and her father Euan, who was in a Scottish regiment."

"And you saw plenty of action," replied a dark-haired man, with the first signs of grey above his ears. He stooped slightly as he spoke to them.

"Yes, sir. Northern Ireland, both wars in Iraq and, just before I left, a tour of Afghanistan." Euan coughed.

Lord Arbemarle ignored it. "Good man. We are indebted to people like you, and I'm delighted to have you as my guest tonight. But will you give me a moment with your daughter?"

Euan raised his eyes at Dotty, who nodded, so he followed Willow towards the front of the box.

Lord Arbemarle turned to Dotty and said, "Willow tells me you're looking for a job, and that you specialise in antiques and police investigations."

Dotty choked on her sparkling water. "I've been learning about antiques, working at an auction house in the Cotswolds. And as for police investigations, they happen by accident."

"I need someone who knows something about paintings and objects of value, but is also organised and able to think independently. You see our curator, Gemma Dunn, is pregnant. Although she's promised to keep working as long as possible, her baby is due in November so she can't possibly organise all of our Christmas extravaganza."

"Which is what?" Dotty asked, trying to sound polite and not too blunt.

"I live at Yoredale Hall in the North Yorkshire Dales, and each year we decorate rooms in the house along a particular theme. I believe this year Gemma has chosen *The Lion, The Witch and the Wardrobe*. I know she's already ordered a large toy lion for the library. We sell packages with lunch or afternoon tea, and visitors arrive by the coach load. The money we raise pays for the annual repairs and keeps us going until the summer tourist season."

Lord Arbemarle sipped his champagne. "I'm looking for someone to organise the Christmas festival and, after it's finished, a deep clean of the entire house, before rearranging the paintings, furniture, and ornaments for display next year. We like to keep it fresh and have something new to attract repeat visitors. And if you have time after that, to continue cataloguing the objects stored in the attics. Who knows what treasures you might find up there hidden away by my ancestors?"

An attic full of treasures did sound exciting, but …

"I can't commit to a full-time job at the moment."

"That's not a problem. In fact, an American gentleman was so desperate for the job that when I turned him down, he insisted on working for free, if we provide him somewhere to stay."

Lord Arbemarle laughed. "One thing we're not short of is bedrooms. You'll have your own ensuite room in the refurbished servants' quarters, and all your meals will be provided. If you'll agree to a six-month contract, to see us through Christmas and the deep clean, I'll pay you £50,000 a month."

That much! And no rent, utility, or food bills. But what about Earl Grey?

"I'm afraid I can't come unless I can bring my cat."

"Is he a mouser?"

Dotty thought back to Earl Grey's regular hunts in France.

"He has been known to chase after mice and small rodents."

"Perfect. An old house like ours is riddled with them, especially when the weather turns cold, and they seek sanctuary indoors. He'll be a welcome addition, as long as he doesn't beg Mrs Briggs for food."

Dotty was certain Earl Grey would try, but it wasn't a reason to reject the job. And how fascinating to work in one of Britain's famous country houses. She'd wanted to visit the Christmas decorations and outdoor lights at Blenheim Palace with her friend, Keya, but they hadn't found the time.

But to organise her own? And perhaps she could invite Keya and her other friends to visit. Her mind returned to the attics. What might she find in them?

She smiled at Lord Arbermarle. "It sounds fascinating. When would you like me to start?"

Holly, Baubles and Murder

Join Dotty, as she and Earl Grey embark on a new chapter in their lives.

But can an exciting role in a remote English country house be a fresh start, or will tragedy strike again?

A joyful Christmas festival turns deadly when a corpse ends up as the chilling centrepiece. Can an amateur sleuth unwrap the tinsel-tangled mystery before the merry cheer melts away?

Claim Your Copy of Holly, Baubles and Murder at
www.books2read.com/HollyBaublesMurder

Earl Grey and Shallow Graves

While Dotty is in France and Edinburgh, crime continues in the Cotswolds. But who will solve the latest mysteries?

Join Dotty's best friend, Sergeant Keya Varma, part time cop and local cafe owner, as she and her colleagues at Cirencester Police Station ensure justice is served, and the Cotswold remain safe.

A 30-year-old skeleton. A missing girl. Can a community police officer read the tea leaves or will a deadly secret remain buried for ever?

Claim Your Copy of Earl Grey and Shallow Graves at
www.books2read.com/EarlGrey

Hour is Come

Would you like to read about Dotty's first case, and discover why she started solving murders and learning about antiques?

Find out and download *Hour is Come,* which is yours to keep when you sign up to my newsletter for updates.

Claim your copy of Hour is Come by visiting VictoriaTait.com

If you enjoyed this book, please tell someone you know. And for those people you don't know, leave a review on Amazon to help them decide whether or not to read it.

For more information visit VictoriaTait.com

Printed in Poland
by Amazon Fulfillment
Poland Sp. z o.o., Wrocław

45007970R00107